Suns of
Magic

Suns of Magic

THE DRAGON CITY

SHANNON ULSIFER / REGINA BEACH

Shannon Ulsifer
P.O. Box 698
Regina Beach, Saskatchewan/S0G 4C0

www.shannonulsifer.com

Publisher's Note: This is a work of fiction. Names, characters, places, and incidents are a product of the author's imagination. Locales and public names are sometimes used for atmospheric purposes. Any resemblance to actual people, living or dead, or to businesses, companies, events, institutions, or locales is completely coincidental.

Book design © 2013, BookDesignTemplates.com

Cover Photography -The Natural Look—Photography by Lavonne Gorrill

Ordering Information: Special discounts are available on quantity purchases by corporations, associations, and others. For details, contact the publisher at the address above.

Shannon Ulsifer — First Edition

ISBN 978-0-9949211-0-9

Printed in the United States of America

For Dad

Prologue

Touching his mother's cold lifeless hand, Roland fought back tears threatening to spill over in an endless splash of cascading water. Sniffling, he walked around the stone slab to stare down at his father. They lay side by side, still, motionless, unresponsive. But somewhere inside the solidity of their stone bodies, their life force remained. Abadon assured him the spell cast by the gargoyles could be reversed, but not until the alignment of the five suns, when the magic of the realm was renewed.

Rubbing the top of his head with both hands, he sighed. Exhaustion swept through his body. It had been an incredibly gruelling, frightening, fantastical night. A night that would be forever etched in his mind. It was the night the fabled creatures came to his home, turned his parents to stone and tried to kidnap him. If not for the warlock Abadon and the medieval knight Sir Balkan, Roland would be in the clutches of the evil dragon Rahm.

Why? The question circled around and around his head like a revolving door, but the answers he had did not stop the spinning. Roland was standing, on his thirteenth birthday, in a secret windowless room of the blue dragon's castle, heartbroken, confused and feeling very much alone. Why did this happen to them? They were a Canadian family, not special in any way, prairie farmers, existing like so many others.

Retreating from the platform of marble his parents lay on, Roland backed away until he felt the cold biting chill of the wall penetrate his weary muscles. Sliding down, he shivered violently as he rested his elbows on his knees and dropped his chin to his chest. He stared at his footsteps marking the dusty floor as though they could supply the answers he so desperately needed to make sense of what happened.

Sensing a fog encroaching upon his drained, fatigued mind, he gave his head an indiscernible shake. It continued, swirling around the edges of his eyes in a blatant attempt to entice him into the serenity of nothingness. He fought with all he had, straining to remain awake. He was so tired, so very tired, weariness filled his body as though it was an empty shell. He would be leaving soon, starting on a quest that may very well end his life. He knew his time with his parents was coming to an end, slipping away much too quickly. He was afraid to leave them, terrified he would never see them again.

Snapping his head up, he focused all his energy on the two prone figures lying together. Staring so intently, he never noticed his eyelids, in miniscule increments, sliding closed. Sleep pressed on him, determined to give him one last moment of rest.   But would it be restful, or full of nightmares?

1

Night of the Gargoyles

First it was the mist, spreading tentacles around his bedroom, searching, feeling, exploring, until discovering him spread out in slumber on his bed, blankets bundled and askew, snoring softly. Confirming the boy was the one they had been searching for, the haze retreated, sucked back by its master.

Roland felt his body shivering with a strange, unwanted summer chill, and sat up groggily, rubbing his eyes. His legs were blindly waging a war with his blankets, trying to untangle them enough to re-cocoon himself inside. Unable to defeat the invisible hands binding the uncooperative covers, he slit his eyes open, trying to identify the problem without opening them fully, unwilling to wake up completely.

Tugging the chaotic layers apart, he kicked his feet like a two year old having a temper tantrum. Flinging himself backward, deciding it was good enough, he lay still waiting for the mythical sandman to send him careening back into his own private dreamland.

The tingles first began in his shoulder blades. Squirming, he turned on his side. They travelled down his spine. He turned to his other side. Ahhh, that was better, they were gone. But were they? Prickles, like he was laying on top of a thorny rose, gathered at the base of his neck before travelling down his spine. And then he froze! Someone was watching him. He could feel the stare, the hair standing up on his neck and arms, an uncanny sense of warning flashed like a neon light behind his eyes. Wanting to turn over and look, but afraid of what was lurking there, he lay motionless, conducting an internal conflict. Look? Don't look? Look? Don't look? Nothing is there. But what if something is?

He was being ridiculous. There was no one in his bedroom. He was getting too old to believe in monsters hiding in the closet or under the bed. It was officially his birthday and he guessed the time to be around two in the morning. He needed to ride this unsubstantiated fear out in true thirteen year old style. He yanked the covers up over his head! Breathing through his mouth, his ears were pealed for any strange sound outside of his makeshift cotton shelter.

Just when he mistakenly considered removing the covers from his head, they were yanked off. Squealing in an embarrassing rendition of a girl, he was dragged out of his bed, pinned between two hideously grotesque creatures, resembling, much to his shock, gargoyles!

Struggling violently, complete and utter terror filled him and he panted, held firmly by cold, living, grey stone hands. There would be no escape this way, the grip like concrete. Taking a deep breath, Plan B formed in his mind in a moment of extreme panic, but before he could execute his scream for help, icy, stubby, rough fingers clamped hard over his mouth.

His bedroom door flew open, revealing another gargoyle creature standing on the threshold. In guttural grunts, he gave undistinguishable orders to his immovable guards, who, with a nod of acknowledgement, proceeded to haul Roland out of his room, down the narrow stairs of the old farmhouse, across the living room, into the porch and outside onto the veranda.

A storm was brewing in the west. Thick, heavy, dark clouds rolled, illuminated by the moon which was valiantly trying to avoid being caught in the tempest about to be unleashed. Thunder rumbled in the distance, while lightning flashed on and off like a poor electrical connection.

"Mom? Dad?" Roland goggled at his parents who stood on the front lawn in their pajamas, flanked by their own personal guards.

"What's going on? What's happening Dad?"

"I don't know Roland, just, do whatever they ask son. Everything will be okay." His father called back. Roland heard the shake in his father's voice. This, more than anything else, planted a lump of dread in his throat. If his dad was scared, Roland knew he should be terrified.

An exceptionally large gargoyle stood just to the side of his parents, and with a loud grunt followed by a jerky wave, Roland's sentinels dragged him down the steps and across the damp grass to deposit him right in front of it. It was obvious to Roland this one was in charge. But what could it possibly want with them? And how were they even here? Gargoyles weren't real. None of this made any sense.

The monstrous creatures came in a grotesque menagerie of shapes and sizes. Roland's eyes travelled over the other four standing off to the side of the leader, noting a tall thin one, two short squat ones and one thick muscular one. All were missing chunks and broken chips from fingers, or faces, arms, legs, feet or shoulders, and their bodies were covered in cracks, deep splits and fractures.

The leader, however, had none. Smooth, grey stone muscles bulged in arms and legs, and a vast chest obliterated everything behind it. Standing seven feet high with large pointed ears, square nose and jutting chin, thick protruding brow and black beady eyes glared maliciously at the three humans. Huge wings rose up from its back, looming outward in the dimness like monstrous bat wings. It was a truly terrifying sight to behold, and Roland shivered with fear. Clawed hands hung loosely at the gargoyle's side, while a leather strap crisscrossed his thick massive chest to join at the bottom and wrap around his waist like a belt. Suspended from it was a black sword as long as Roland's body.

Snarling, it crossed its arms, its stance one of complete authority. Roland tilted his head back to look up into its face. Black, beady, lidless eyes glared down at him. Sharp pointed teeth shone sickeningly in the moonlight, as the creature smiled, callous and malicious intent obvious. It looked like a prehistoric creature and Roland would never ever forget that face!

"What do you want from us? Why are you here? Where do you come from?" Camedon White struggled against the clawed hands holding him. "You made a mistake! We are nothing to you! Let us go. No one needs to know you were ever here." He bartered, desperate to save his family. Tall and wiry, he was stronger than he looked, but he was unable to even loosen the grip on his arm, let alone break free.

"Please, please, just let us go!" Roland's mother Jilleesa cried out. A housewife and mother, she was slight in stature, dwarfed by the gargoyle holding her arm in a tight painful grip, while her housecoat flapped in the wind, heralding the rapid approach of the storm.

The next five minutes was a fast forward blur in Roland's mind. One of the gargoyles handed the leader a stick with a small dragon shaped skull on top, the inside lit with a dim orange glow. The effect was creepy and ghostly, like a Halloween costume prop. Pointing the snout of the dragon at first his father and then his mother, Roland roared in shock as a flash of orange light blasted out of the dragon's mouth, and his parents, one at a time, turn to stone right where they stood.

Letting them fall backwards with a thud onto the ground, their guards hopped around in glee, pleased at the outcome. Spitefully, they kicked dirt and grass on them.

"Stop it!" Roland yelled, trying desperately to break free of the cement like fingers of steel. "Let me go!" Kicking at the leader, Roland's vision blurred with the tears flooding down his face. "What did you do to them? What did you do? You dirty rotten pile of rock!"

Roland squawked when the leader, with an unimaginable speed, shoved his face down into Roland's. Roland froze in terror, unconsciously holding his breath. The creature growled, gnashing pointed teeth, causing tiny pebbles to spray Roland like saliva. Jerking his head back, the creature smiled nastily before raising a single long, black claw, resting it against Roland's face, just below his eye. Pressing painfully, he punished Roland for his outburst slicing a thin line down his cheek. Tiny beads of blood formed, trickling down. The gargoyle chuckled ruthlessly at Roland's gasp of pain. And then the chuckle changed into a raw, liquid gurgle. Surprise crossed its face as it dropped its hand from Roland's cheek and stretched itself up, turning around. Roland's eyes widened when he saw a blue and silver sword sticking out between the gargoyle's shoulder blades, centered between its wings. Black liquid poured out in rivets and the gargoyle fell face first into the grass.

Wings unfurled and flapped as the others rose up into the air, confused and frightened, searching for the culprit who killed their leader. Roland's guard let him go to follow the rest, and Roland ran over to his parents, kneeling in the grass beside his mother, touching her cold hand, calling her name, receiving no response.

Scanning the area, Roland tried to find the person responsible for killing that horrid creature, but all he saw was a small, blue glowing ball of light launched out of the darkness beyond the yard light to connect with one rising gargoyle. Another followed immediately, catching a second gargoyle and both plunged to the ground with a thud, wings at unnatural angles, unmoving, dead. Two more plummeted, hit by the same deadly objects, while another two creatures crashed into each other in their panic, sending chunks of stone spewing in all directions, spiraling them down to meet the earth. Two others grew smaller and smaller, escaping into the night sky.

Wide eyed and intent on what was happening, Roland didn't realize two remaining gargoyles had crept around behind him. Roland yelped when clawed fingers suddenly clasped his shoulders. The sound of flapping wings filled the night as Roland's feet left the ground.

"Help, help! Somebody help me!" Roland shouted, squirming wildly, making it difficult for them to lift him up any higher, his legs kicking, his shoulders bucking and his arms flailing. He was like a flopping fish out of water, and the two gargoyles had to keep adjusting their grip in order to hang on.

Two figures stepped out of the darkness into the faint circle of light. One, a knight, while the other looked like he was a genie who just emerged from Aladdin's lamp. The gargoyles released Roland and he tumbled to the ground. Shrieking and gurgling in anger, they attacked the newcomers. Roland rubbed his eyes in disbelief, as he watched the knight dispose of his opponent with three masterful parries and thrusts of his sword. The other guard was scattered to the wind in pieces and pebbles when defeated by the genie, who was swinging some kind of stick or staff.

Rising from the ground, Roland swayed on his feet, the world around him fading into blurry shadows. The knight pointed his sword at Roland's chest, muffled words came from moving lips, but Roland didn't know if he was talking to him or about him. It was as though he was viewing it from under water with everything distorted and inaudible. He never felt the strong, muscular arms catch him before he hit the ground.

2

The Timekeeper

Two figures stood over the unconscious boy, one frowning, the other deep in thought.

"Are we sure he is the one we have been looking for?" The knight pointed at the unconscious boy with the tip of his sword, his silver armor and chain mail colliding together like metal wind chimes. The knight shifted his silver shield, emblazoned with a blue dragon, hooking it to his shoulder, swinging it back, concealing it under the black cape that flashed a blue shimmery lining with each small gust of wind.

"Five hundred years, search, we have. Find him we did. Just in time we were." The other replied.

"Yeah, just in time. How did Rahm happen to find him at the exact same time as we did? I don't believe in coincidences like that Abadon. I think we need to be very careful." The knight thrust his sword into the ground, leaning on it with both hands wrapped around the handle protectively.

"Careful?"

"Yes, careful. I think we may have a traitor in our midst."

Abadon's silver eyebrows angled up in surprise.

"Oh come on, don't tell me it didn't cross your mind as well. I smelled a traitor when the Timekeeper was stolen three weeks ago. Only someone on the inside would know the best time to have access to the Timekeeper, and that was during the summer solstice celebration. Chara leaves his castle only a few times a year, and the solstice is one of those times. The theft was very well planned and executed."

"Know we do, Kentor stole the Timekeeper," Abadon argued.

"Yeah, but I don't think he did it alone. He had to have help. He hadn't been in Katori long enough to pull it off without someone masterminding the plan. I'm telling you Abadon, Rahm has someone working for him on the inside." The knight tore the sword out of the ground, wiping the end of the blade on his forearm before slamming it back into its blue and silver scabbard. Frustration evident in his determined movements.

A groan from the boy halted conversation.

"Mom? Dad?" Roland sat up with their names on his lips. Blinking, he looked around in confusion. "What happened? Where am I? Who are you guys?" Roland asked when his eyes focused on the two figures standing above him.

"Abadon I am," said the genie with a slight bow.

"And I am Sir Balkan, Knight of the Realm of Abraxas."

The man calling himself Abadon wore billowing blue pants with bands at the ankles. The waist, to just above the knee, was covered by thick, white material embroidered along the edges in the same striking blue with tassels that dripped off the bottom. Silver arm cuffs circled forearms, while silver and blue braided rope crisscrossed his wrists almost to his elbows. A wide blue belt circled his waist, where colorful trinkets, ornaments and charms dangled. A braided whip hung from his right hip and a small round wooden stick fell from the other. A thick silver chain circled his neck where a round silver pendant, engraved with a blue dragon, lay on his chest. One ear was draped in chains secured along the rim and pinned together at the lobe. Muscles rippled, his six foot seven countenance impressive, and a silver goatee was being stroked by long, thin fingers. But what Roland starred at unabashedly was the man's navy colored skin which was covered in white swirls and symbols. Every speck, even his bald head, was filled with markings, like Michelangelo had used his navy skin as a master canvas. He was truly the most impressive being Roland had ever seen.

Roland's eyes darted from one to the other, before coming back to the one standing at his feet. "Whoa, are you like a genie?" he breathed in awe, saying the first thing that came to his mind.

"Warlock, I am," Abadon said in a soft, smooth, honey voice.

It was too unbelievable and needing time to gather his thoughts, Roland looked away and then around, realizing he was laying on long, soft purple grass. He really couldn't be awake yet, he must still be dreaming, dreaming he was awake. Yeah, that must be it, his mind unwilling to accept all he had seen, needing to create another explanation. Standing up, he swiped at the blades stuck to his legs while avoiding any further eye contact.

Taking a deep breath, he realized he couldn't go any further until he knew for sure. Gathering up his courage he asked the most important question of his life. "Am I, uh, well…. dreaming?"

"No, Roland White, dreaming you are not." The warlock replied softly.

Roland's eyes burned and tears threatened. He didn't want to cry in front of these guys, but he felt confused, scared and sick, his stomach rolled like a boat bobbing on uncontrolled waves. He wanted his mom and dad. He wanted to know what happened to them and if they were okay. Words stuck in the back of his throat like a chicken bone. Swallowing with tremendous effort, he stared at the ground, both mesmerized and lost in the flowing purple threads of grass as they waved and danced with not a care in the world.

"Understand, I do. Afraid you are. Parents turned to stone by gargoyle. At my master's castle they are. Enough magic to send only them, there was. Save them I can. See them you will. To Abraxas we go."

Abadon spoke softly to the forlorn looking boy.

Raising his head slowly, afraid to hope, Roland asked, "My parents are okay?"

Sighing, Abadon looked at Sir Balkan, who only shrugged in response. The motion conveying silent words, "you're on your own here."

"Made of stone they are. Statues they be. Fix them we can, but your help we need."

"My help? But what can I do to help? Where did the gargoyles come from and how were they alive and why did they turn my parents to stone and…?" His questions were halted in his throat like they hit a wall when the warlock raised a hand.

"Beginning I will start. Not much time. Questions later. Agreed?"

"Yeah okay."

"Much to explain." Abadon began pacing, leaving a flattened purple trail of footsteps. Stopping suddenly, he returned to Roland. "Show you I will. Faster, easier," he said reaching out his navy and white swirl covered hands.

"Wait a second," Roland said, backing up. "What are you doing?"

"Trust me. Show you I will."

"It's okay kid. Let him touch you. It will be faster than trying to explain everything. We have to get going. We don't want to be sitting here if the gargoyles come back now do we?" Sir Balkan crossed his arms, raising an eyebrow at Roland.

Transferring his weight from foot to foot, Roland tugged at the hem of his white undershirt. "Alright, but it's not gonna hurt is it?"

"Hurt you it will not." Reaching forward, Abadon placed his hands on either side of Roland's head, just above his ears. Taking a deep breath, Roland closed his eyes when Abadon whispered the instructions for him to do so.

Silence filled his world and then pictures began forming in his mind, like short movies.

First he saw five spheres in the sky, yellow, blue, green, pink and black. In a perfect line, each burst apart, one after the other, sending effervescent particles exploding outward like opening a gigantic can of pop. The luminous particles churned and rolled together, creating a massive, incandescent gleaming cloud. The entire sky was resplendent in glowing, glittering miniscule stars. Dancing wildly, they began to rotate together, faster and faster and faster, until a tornado like funnel filled the atmosphere.

Spinning wildly, almost ferociously, the tornado hovered for a moment in the sky, before being sucked down to the earth. Roland's mind was transported into a white marble room, where the dazzling stars were being drawn into a floating hourglass that was almost the size of Roland. It was wrapped in vines, leaves and flowers and a large white dragon stood behind it, his arms and head were raised to the opening above and his wings were spread out as he seemed to direct the whirlwind of tiny stars into the hourglass.

The particles were sucked into the hourglass and when the top half was full of the miniscule shimmering stars, the white dragon leaned over to blow softly on the glass and then slumped to the floor, closed his eyes and lay still. With that breath, tiny sparkling stars began to flow in a small steady stream from the top to the bottom of the hourglass.

Roland was shown the same room, but now the white dragon was gone and something else was happening. The room was gradually filling up with a heavy black mist, gliding in from all sides until the hourglass was first surrounded, and then completely shielded from view. A small, dark dragon shape formed in the mist, and when the mist receded, the dragon form and the hourglass was gone!

Abadon removed his hands and Roland saw a blue glow fading away from the white markings on the warlock's hands.

"Understand you did?"

"Yeah, I think so. Those tiny stars went into an hourglass, where they started falling down to the bottom, kind of like a sands of time thing, and then it disappeared, like it was stolen, but what was that hourglass thingy?"

"Timekeeper it is called. It is the *Magic of Time*, magic collected from universe, released by suns alignment every five thousand years. New alignment approaches. Timekeeper stolen by Rahm. Control magic he will try. Master of realm his goal. Bad for all it is. Come, go now we must. To Abraxas." Turning quickly he waved his hands over an area above the grass and layers of chipped, stone steps appeared from nowhere. They led up to a large stone archway. Fragments of mortar lay strewn on the ground revealing the ancient age of the arch.

With a nod from Abadon, Roland took a first hesitant step up, feeling a bit braver when the other two joined him.

3

Crossing Over

Step after step, the three figures trudged upward until finally reaching a landing at the top. There they faced the archway and Roland raised his eyebrows in surprise. The entrance was filled with thick wavering water. It was as though it was being detained by an invisible wall, with multi colored ribbons draped inside, suspended and unmoving like someone paused the TV remote.

Looking up at Abadon questioningly, Abadon looked over Roland's head to Sir Balkan, giving a nod. Turning his head to the knight, Roland watched as Sir Balkan stepped through the water barrier. His image quickly wavered and distorted, stretching him out like a fun mirror at the fair. First he was long and skinny, curving sideways, and then he was three feet tall and six feet wide, every feature misshapen. Roland gasped and stepped backwards. "What's happening to him?"

"Fine he is. Balkan," Abadon called, and the knight exited the watery wall to stand in front of Roland, everything back to normal. He looked the same as he did before he went in.

"Come on, let's hurry this up," he said impatiently. "We don't have all day. Let's go kid. It isn't going to hurt you!" Turning he returned to the water, his elongated form faded away after a few steps.

Abadon walked in next and his form stretched too, but the warlock continued walking and his form dwindled away until Roland couldn't see him.

Looking around, Roland realized he had no choice. There was really nowhere else to go. He had no idea where he was and in looking behind, he saw the archway and steps had disappeared, revealing more water behind him. It was like standing in the middle of a swimming pool with walls of water on both sides and a single dry spot in the centre. Realizing his only choice was to go forward, he tentatively reach out a hand, touching the water. It felt like a thick, gooey gel. He hoped he was gonna be able to breathe in there.

Lifting his foot up, he stuck it into the gel-like water. He could feel a resistance on his foot, like trying to step through rubber, but as he followed through on the step, his body entered and he was inside. He did it! This was soooo cool, he thought. It was like being wrapped in a really, really soft, warm blanket. He could breathe just fine, and he tested the gel by raising an arm. It was like moving in slow motion, the thickness of the water created enough pressure that he had to try harder to move.

The ribbons appeared, moving toward him in a slow swimming motion. Standing stock still, Roland held his breath as they approached. Closer and closer they came, until the first red ribbon reached him. It began wrapping itself around him and Roland felt a moment of panic, before it released him. Returning, it came back and did it again, as though gently surrounding him in soft caresses. More came, yellow ones and green ones, pink ones and orange ones. A weird tingling sensation arose wherever the ribbons touched, as though they were exploring and searching, conducting their own investigation on this strange intruder of their world. At first he tried to remove them as they slithered around his body, but realizing it was a lost cause because there were too many, he gave up. Besides, they weren't harming him in any way, so he decided to leave them alone.

Ahead, he could make out the shapes of Abadon and Sir Balkan, who had halted, obviously waiting for him. The pressure of the gel forced him to move slowly, but he eventually reached the other two. Stopping beside Abadon, the ribbons untangled themselves from his body to float ahead and join what was already a large number of them hanging down in front of them like curtains. Abadon's hand markings glowed a soft light blue, and he waved it across the ribbons. They slowly parted in the middle, revealing more stairs behind.

His eyes followed wide stairs cut into a mountainside rising up as far as his eyes could see. Small flowing streams of water ran on either side of the stairs, flanked by a railing.

Stepping out of the gel onto the first step, Sir Balkan and Abadon began the climb, and shrugging Roland followed. After a few steps, he looked back, surprised to see nothing but more steps. The ribbons and gel-like water were gone. The view now contained nothing but more stairs that continued down the mountain until lost from view in a gathering fog below. Roland wondered why they were going up instead of down, and curiosity had him thinking about what could be found at the bottom. Maybe there wasn't a bottom? Maybe the stairs went down forever, like holes in the earth where there seemed to be no end.

"Uh, excuse me, mister warlock sir." Roland called up to the warlock who was a few steps ahead of him.

Not looking back and not stopping, the warlock replied, "Just Abadon, and yes?"

"Oh, okay, uh Abadon. I was just wondering why that big gargoyle didn't turn me to stone like he did to my mom and dad."

"Not turn you to stone. Need you they do. Take you away they would."

"Take me away? You mean they were trying to kidnap me?"

"Yes."

"But why?" Roland was astounded at the information. On the outside he seemed to be going with the flow, but inside his stomach was filled with butterflies and his mind spun in circles. Where was he? Why did all this happen? Was it real or was he dreaming? And on and on it went, an internal dialogue of unanswered questions.

Another step and another and another, until wincing, Roland stopped. The roughness of the steps was cutting the bottom of his feet. He was after all, still in his boxer shorts and undershirt. He had no shoes, no pants, jacket etc. Taking another step, he winced again, louder this time.

Abadon stopped and turned around, looking down at Roland.

Raising an eyebrow when Roland met his eyes, his unspoken inquiry was all Roland needed.

Grabbing the rail, he raised his leg so Abadon could see the bottom of his scratched up foot. "You got an extra pair of shoes on you by chance?" he asked.

Abadon raised his hands and Roland could see the markings light up with that soft blue light. The next thing Roland knew, his feet were covered in soft brown leather moccasins.

"Hey, these aren't girls shoes are they?" he asked, because they kinda looked like shoes girls would wear. Abadon ignored the question and started to turn away to resume the climb.

"Uhhh, sir, do you think you could uh, give me some clothes too. I'm really kinda over running around in my underwear."

Turning back, unable to control a small smirk, Abadon raised his hands once again, the swirls and symbols lighting up, before he gave them a sharp clap.

Looking down, Roland saw his legs covered in tan colored pants and his white shirt was replaced with a long sleeved, black, collarless shirt. The sleeves were wide and billowy and strings laced together at his neckline like shoelaces on runners.

Rolling his shoulders, he felt much better, less exposed.

"Thank you sir," he said with relief.

"Welcome you are."

Turning, Abadon continued up the steps, and Roland followed. Abadon's magic was amazing and he wouldn't have believed any of it if he hadn't witnessed it with his own eyes. He was with a real live warlock. In other circumstances, it would be the coolest thing to ever happen to him. But right now, all he could really focus on was getting wherever it was they were going so that he could see his parents again.

Rubbing the tops of his thighs, he sighed. His legs were getting tired, the muscles straining and weary. Looking up, he figured they were about three quarters of the way. Man what a long trek!

Letting his thoughts float away, the repetitive movement of climbing the stairs lulled him into an empty thoughtless void. A large shadow crossed over the sun, blocking the light. What was that? His attention snapped back to reality. Viewing the sky, Roland caught sight of a large bird, just as it swooped down at him. Reflexes had him ducking and the bird turned and circled back for another swipe, dropping low. Roland saw another join the first, the pterodactyl size disturbing and threatening. Making a crisscross swoop in the sky, Roland was astonished to realize they weren't birds after all. They were gargoyles!

"Sssirrr," Roland whispered in terror, desperately trying to find his voice, fear blocking the sound. "A-Abadon," he said a bit louder before the name burst from his vocal cords in a tremendous shout, "ABADONNNNN!"

Turning nimbly on the steps, Abadon barked a word at Sir Balkan, and steel screeched as the knight swiftly drew his sword. Racing down the steps, Roland's rescuers stood, one below him and one above him, their sole purpose, to protect Roland.

One gargoyle plunged downward, claws projecting outward, intent on ripping the warlock to shreds, or better yet, fling him down the rocky steps, but his momentum was halted when the warlock snapped the stick off his belt and with a single downward swipe, turned it into a long, solid, wooden staff. Jabbing it forward in a blur of motion, he stabbed the gargoyle in the midsection, causing a woof of air to explode out of its lungs at the same moment as it began somersaulting wildly downward. Using its wings to reclaim its balance, it charged back up, skimming the steps with bat-like wings, deadly intent filling its squashed, broken face.

Legs spread for stability, Abadon faced his foe, his staff twirling in his hand, whirring like a helicopter blade. When the gargoyle was close enough, Abadon bashed it on the head, eliciting a grunt before smacking it under the chin with a resounding whack. Falling with a thud on the steps, the creature flopped down the stairs, one at a time, until it disappeared into the thick fog far below.

Sir Balkan, who was standing behind Roland, reached down, snagged him by his shirt and hauled him right up off his feet to plunk him down directly behind him. Roland wobbled back and forth on the step before regaining his balance. Facing the second gargoyle, Sir Balkan thrust and jabbed with his sword, while the gargoyle zipped nimbly out of the way.

The knight was engrossed in his battle, while Abadon faced a third, no one noticed a fourth creature sneak in behind Roland.

Roland felt sharp talons dig into his shoulders and shouted in fear. Razor sharp claws broke fabric covered skin and blood trickled from each piercing. Roland squirmed in pain, instinct kicked in and he struggled, swinging and flailing his arms, scratching and tearing at the gargoyle. Feeling his body rising up off the step, he reached over and grabbed the top of the railing, hanging on for his life. Straining forward, he managed to completely wrap his arms around the wooden lifeline, practically laying on top of it, his teeth gritted against painful jerks, as the gargoyle tried to dislodge him from his death grip with heaving pulls. Tearing his claws from Roland's skin, he landed to the side of the railing, wrapping cold, hard arms around Roland's waist. Pulling and tugging, it held him in an awkward hug, trying to pick him off like he was a sticky piece of gum.

"Let go of me!" Roland screamed at it, kicking sideways. Roland felt his arms weakening. He wasn't going to be able to hang on much longer as the gargoyle was much stronger than he was. With one last wrenching pull, Roland's hold on the rail was broken and he found himself being held, his back tight against the iciness of its stone chest.

A fifth gargoyle landed in front of Roland, its wings guiding it to a standing position two steps below. Bringing in its grey stone-like wings, black beady eyes were level with

Roland's and it glared down its beak-like nose at him. Roland stared at the missing chunk of stone on the end of it. Glowering at Roland in disgust, like he was a disease, corn on the cob shaped ears twitched back and forth, while its front claws reached out toward him. Turning his head sideways, Roland looked away. He couldn't bear to watch what was about to happen. It was going to rip him apart! Bracing himself for the pain to come, he waited... and waited. Nothing happened!

Opening his eyes, he was just in time to see Sir Balkan with a stranglehold around its neck. Stepping sideways, Sir Balkan gave a great heave, sending it backward, its wings flailing as it tried to stop its downward trajectory. Sir Balkan gave it a single hard kick to the chest and the creature tumbled end over end. Down it went, cries of pain stopped suddenly, leaving only thudding noises, until they too ceased.

Roland gave his body a quick jerky sideways twist and the creature behind him, unprepared for it, lost its grip. Roland was free. Taking a huge step to the side he grabbed the safety of the railing once again as Sir Balkan leaped up to stand between Roland and the creature, swinging the flat side of his sword across the creature's head. The force of the swing knocked the gargoyle out cold and it crumpled like paper before sailing down the steps, joining its comrades below.

One last gargoyle remained. Flapping its wings, it lifted itself up in the air, wondering how it was going to retrieve the boy, afraid to return to its master without him. As it rose, a great whoosh sounded as Abadon swung his staff with deadly accuracy, knocking the beast on one of its wings with a telltale crack. It tried to fly, fluttering up and down, the wing hanging useless as the creature screeched in pain. It landed awkwardly and off balance on the steps. Abadon raced down, planted his staff on the step and raising his body in the air, swung around the staff, both feet connecting with the jaw of the gargoyle. Landing nimbly, Abadon watched as this one too fell, down, down, down.

Silence filled the air, broken only by Roland's harsh breathing. What did these things want with him and were there more? He wasn't the only one thinking that, as he saw Abadon and Sir Balkan carefully inspecting the sky.

He plunked himself down on the step, his hands and legs shaking. Abadon and Sir Balkan had saved his life. Again.

Staring down below, Roland's blood ran cold. The steps, the railing and the water were disappearing. It looked like everything below them was made of dominoes, and someone had set one off, starting a chain reaction. The stairs, water and railing were rolling upwards, leaving behind nothing but the rocky terrain of a very steep mountain side.

Crap, crap and double crap, Roland thought.

"Move we must, now!" cried Abadon, as he too saw the steps folding up. "Realm path closing!"

Roland stood, turned and ran up those steps as fast as his rubbery legs could carry him, but he wasn't fast enough. Abadon grabbed him around the waist and hoisted him up under an arm. His head bounced up and down like a rubber ball as the warlock took the steps three at a time as though carrying nothing more than a feather. Looking down, Roland saw the steps blur as his feet continued pumping frantically in midair. Reaching the last step, Abadon lowered Roland onto a large flat outcropping, not even breathing heavy in the cold mountain air.

Seconds later, the last step clicked as it set itself back into the mountain. There were no more steps, no water and no railing, just rocks, moss, brush and some thin yellow trees, their roots holding onto the side of the mountain, forcing the trees to grow out at an awkward angle.

Whew! They made it, and just in time too. Roland was incredibly relieved that all the danger and excitement was finally over.

4

The Hall of Dragons

Roland wondered where they were
now. Obviously getting to this
realm place wasn't a simple process.
Sir Balkan was panting, leaning over with his
hands on his knees. "I'm getting to old for
this," he wheezed.

Roland giggled. Not that it was really
funny, it was more of a stress reliever, but the
responding half smile, half grimace from Sir
Balkan made Roland feel slightly better.

It was only when Abadon began speaking
in his strange soft, choppy way, that Roland
realized they weren't alone. Two figures,
covered head to toe in brown robes, hoods
obscuring their faces, stood guard on either
side of a jumbled pile of rocks. Heads
bowed, they listened carefully to Abadon,

who was advising them of the gargoyle attack.

Nodding, they pulled small sticks out of their sleeves and with quick movements, turned them into long staffs identical to Abadon's. If they could use them as well as Abadon, Roland thought, they would be safe.

With a quick nod of satisfaction, Abadon turned to the massive pile of rocks on the outcropping. Raising glowing hands, he began speaking softly, strange magical words floated in the air. The landslide of rocks began moving, sliding and shifting in all directions. Dust particles filled the air, and Roland coughed, waving his hand in front of his face. The noise of the grinding rocks was deafening, and when the dust finally cleared and he could see again, Roland was astounded to see the rocky outcropping had reformed into a colossal stone dragon head. It looked as though it had been carved out of the mountain, the detail so exquisite it could be alive. How on earth did that pile of rock turn into this amazing dragon?

But Abadon wasn't quite done yet, and raising his arms, arms, hands and chest lit with glowing markings, Abadon called out one word as he waved his hands in a crisscross pattern in the air, "Aperi!"

A deep muffled rumble vibrated the ground beneath their feet. Pebbles and dust sprayed into the air like an exploding volcano. Roland's mouth dropped open as he watched the dragon mouth begin to move! Taking a step backward in shock, he immediately realized his mistake. His move had taken him to the edge of the ledge, his heel dangling over into the vastness below. His arms swung wildly as he desperately tried to regain his balance, as his back curved into that foggy void as gravity pulled at his body, intent on sending him over into the abyss. He was going to fall!

Before he could scream out in terror, his heart falling to his stomach, Abadon flung his arm back toward Roland without turning his head, his hand and arm glowing a brilliant white, the markings decorated the air above as it shone out of the warlock's skin. Roland felt a magnetic pull forcing him forward, first one step and then another and another, until he was safely away from the death drop.

Falling to his knees, Roland clasped his hands together behind his head and rocked back and forth trying to get his heart to return to his chest from his stomach. Swiping his hands down his face, he left dirty streaks behind while cold sweat stung his eyes. Using the bottom of his shirt, he wiped his forehead and expelled an enormous breath. Refilling his lungs, he held the precious air in, trying to stop the wild thudding of his heart.

"That was a close one kid. You gotta watch what you're doing." The knight said watching him.

"Yeah no kidding. Roger that one." Leaning back on his knees, he looked up at Sir Balkan. "Abadon is amazing. Can everyone do magic like that where you're from? Can you?"

"No, I can't, and no, not everyone can, but most rely on it in some way."

Abadon interrupted. "Time it is to enter. Come Roland White."

"Enter what?"

"The Realm of Abraxas."

"Yeah, okay, no problem." Roland replied with sarcasm, like travelling from realm to realm was no big deal. Rising slowly to his feet, he pointed at the now, wide open, stone dragon mouth, "Let me guess, we have to go in there right? Yeah, sure we do, because just having a good old regular door that we could open and close would be asking too much. You know, it's been one thing after another and I've had just about all I can take!" Roland almost shouted in frustration. Every crazy, unbelievable thing that had happened so far, ending with him almost falling to his death, had taken him to the end of his rope. He wanted to go home, crawl back into his bed and wake up to find it had all been a dream.

"What he saying?" Abadon looked at Sir Balkan for help, clearly lost in the wake of the boy's firestorm of babbling words.

Smacking Abadon on the shoulder as he walked by, Sir Balkan clarified, "he's saying he is now going to become a thirteen year old pain in the....."

"Hey that's not fair!" Roland interrupted. "I did not...," but his voice trailed off when Sir Balkan burst out laughing. Abadon looked from one to the other, thoroughly confused.

"Just kidding kid. You needed to snap out of the pity party you were having. You've done a great job so far. Heck, you've even amazed me, so don't give up now. Remember that you're parents need you. Now, come on, let's get moving. Buck up boy, you've only seen a little, get ready to see a whole lot more."

"Yeah, yeah," Roland mumbled, but secretly, he was pleased with the praise from the knight.

Sir Balkan swung away from Roland and entered the dragon's mouth, turning sideways to squeeze past giant teeth that rose up over the knight's head, and without looking back, disappeared into the darkness beyond, swallowed whole by the gaping mouth.

5

Eltanin

Roland entered the dragon's mouth filled with apprehension. Passing the teeth, he moved slowly to the back of the throat, passing through and into a cave. Squinting in the darkness, Roland thought he detected movement ahead. Yes, there is was again! What the heck was that? Uh oh, it's a shadow! A shadow of what? Another gargoyle or some other dangerous creature out to get him?

Oh, it was just Sir Balkan. Sheesh, was he getting paranoid or what!

A loud screeching noise caught his attention. He turned in time to see the enormous dragon mouth closing, swallowing them, sealing them inside.

The darkness was now as thick as syrup. Large torches came to life along both sides of the wall and Roland realized they weren't in a cave after all, but rather a tunnel cut right through the mountain. Dancing shadows rose up from each flame. The flickering light revealed Sir Balkan way ahead of them now. Inspecting the walls, the dancing flames revealed incredible meticulously chiseled pictures on the surface of the surrounding walls. Roland's eyes roamed along the contours of the lines and curves trying to understand what he was looking at. Reaching out, his fingers traced the smooth contours. He was just about to ask Abadon what they were pictures of when his eyes widened. They were detailed, exquisitely carved dragons, surrounded by what looked like cryptic words, signs and symbols. His fingers continued their inspection when another connection was made.

"Hey," exclaimed Roland, "some of that stuff on the wall is the same as the markings you have on your uh, skin, er, body, sir!" he cried in astonishment.

"Indeed."

"That is so awesome! What are they, I mean, the markings. What do they mean?"

"Dragon language it be. Earned it I have. Many years of study with my Master. Access to dragon magic it is."

"Whoa…" Roland breathed, unable to say anything more.

"Almost at Abraxas we are. Come, time later," he commanded Roland, before turning away.

Roland tore his eyes from the walls wanting more time to look at the carvings. He wished he had his cell phone because he would have taken a gazillion pictures of them. They were so cool.

Abadon turned and started down the hall after Sir Balkan.

"Uh, sir, why are there dragons on the wall anyway?" Roland asked, giving the walls one last wistful look before jogging after the warlock.

Not pausing, Abadon answered, "Abadon good."

Roland scrunched up his face. What did that mean? Then he got it. Abadon only wanted to be called Abadon, not sir. "Okay, uh Abadon, what is this place exactly?"

"Hall of Dragons this is." Abadon's voice echoed eerily, bouncing off the stone.

Roland trotted a few steps again to catch up. Jeez, walking with this guy was worse than running football laps.

"Oh," replied Roland, because that just explained everything! Wiping the sweat off his forehead, he prepared to try again. "But..."

Abadon paused while Roland was in the middle of another quick two steps to catch up. He passed the warlock. Halting, he turned, looking up questioningly.

Looking down at Roland, Abadon put his hands behind his back, lacing his fingers together. A thoughtful expression filled his face, before a hand reappeared to stroke his silver goatee absently. Quiet for a moment, Abadon then resumed walking, slower this time, and began to speak.

"Many millennia older our realm is than your world," he said. "Writing on walls, dragon language it be. Story of Dragon Masters' it tells. Reign for many of your lifetimes, they do. Care, nurture and keep safe our realm. Gateway curtain between worlds we passed. Secret stairs we climb. Hall we travel now. Realm of Abraxas at other end," Abadon indicated with a wave of his arm the glimmer of light Roland could see at the other end. "Only one from prophecy can save it."

"A prophecy? That is so sweet? Save what? The realm? Who is going to save it?"

"Yes, realm. Grave danger it is in. You. You, Roland White, the chosen one from prophecy to save realm!"

Roland started laughing. "That's really funny. But really," he said between chuckles, "what's happening with the realm? Why is it in danger?"

His laughter faded away at Abadon's steely stare.

"What? Seriously? Aw come on, you're just messing with me. Why would some old prophecy talk about me? That's just ridiculous. I mean, how do I know I'm not actually in a hospital somewhere in a coma? Or even still, at home in my bed sleeping like a baby, dreaming all this up?"

Abadon reached out so quickly Roland didn't see it coming and gave a yelp when he felt a quick, sharp pain on his upper arm.

"What the? Hey, did you just pinch me?" Roland asked, rubbing his arm briskly.

"Is only way show you not dreaming," Abadon smirked.

"Okay, okay I get it, it's not a dream. Next time can you like, maybe just say so? That hurt!"

"No. Miss fun of pinch then."

Rolling his eyes, Roland followed when Abadon turned to continue down the great hallway.

They hadn't gone very far when Roland, after all those steps up the mountain and now the long hike down the Hall of Dragons, realized how exhausted he was.

"Do you think we could stop for a minute Abadon? I am done for."

"Done for what?" Abadon raised a questioning eyebrow down at Roland.

"What?" asked Roland, feeling confused.

"What?" Abadon replied, now also confused.

Staring at the warlock for a second, Roland said slowly, "I mean, or meant, that I am beat."

"Beat," Abadon repeated. "Beat you no one did!" he said indignantly.

"No, no," Roland tried to explain, "I mean I'm tired!"

"Oh. Yes, believe this be true. Here," Abadon waved his hand in the air, magically producing a small etched glass jar that was full of black liquid. "Sip this. Remove your fatigue it will."

"Ewwww, that looks disgusting," Roland wrinkled up his nose. "I'm not drinking that!"

"Feel better yes or no?" Abadon asked, running out of patience.

"Well, yeah, I do, but I'm still not drinking that!" he pointed at the small jar.

Abadon eyeballed Roland with a fierce look before it drained away and he sighed. "Very well." The jar vanished and he reached toward Roland with one hand, the trademark soft blue glow illuminating the white markings. Roland knew it meant Abadon was going to perform some kind of magic. It got closer and closer to his face.

"Hey, just a second," Roland yelped, ducking to avoid Abadon's reaching hand.

"Hurt you I will not. If no elixir, then touch. Better feel you will." Raising a silver eyebrow, he taunted, "scared you are?"

Pulling himself up to his full five feet, he said, "I am not scared, and don't you mean, *to make me feel better*," Roland corrected. Abadon only inclined his head. The challenge had been issued, however, and Roland wasn't backing down from it.

Once again reaching out, Abadon rested his hand on the top of Roland's head.

A slight tingle at the same time as Abadon whispered a mysterious word, and Roland felt an instant warmth spread through his body and it felt amazing! Every sore muscle, ache and pain was gone! Even the scratch on his cheek from the big gargoyle disappeared.

He couldn't supress a groan of pleasure. "That was awesome! How do you do that?" Roland asked, testing out all his body parts, shaking his legs and moving his arms around as he walked. He quit when he realized he probably looked like he was having a seizure or even worse, doing the chicken dance. The light faded away and Abadon crossed his arms, causing the biceps to bulge out. "Magic it is Roland White."

"But how did you get that magic? How do you make it work?"

"You like small bird chittering in ear. Take break, stop chittering."

Roland smirked. "Well, don't forget, you are the one who dragged me here. Now, are we almost there yet? I want to see my parents."

"Yes, almost there. Come."

"You didn't answer my question about that prophecy thingy."

"Questions do you ever stop asking?"

"Nope. I am on a need to know basis, and I need to know everything!"

"Not need to know all right now. No patience, just question, question, question. Chatter, chatter, chatter. Headache you give me."

"Phht."

Abadon's face filled with surprise. "Did you "phht" me?"

Roland's mouth dropped open.

"Close mouth you should! If open wider, swally crawl in! And Roland, don't ever phht me again. Great warlock I am, disrespectful that is."

Roland closed his mouth. Crossing his arms, he tilted his head to look at Abadon out of the corner of his eye. "Well that just sounds gross! What is a swally? Are you still teasing or is that true? And thanks, by the way, for making me feel better with your magical warlock hands. And I'm sorry, I won't phht you again. But just so as you know, that doesn't mean I might not phht someone else."

Nodding in satisfaction, Abadon explained. "Very disgusting swally is. Thousands of legs it has. Black and green, long, slimy. Make nests in warm places, like wide open mouth! Yes, is true and welcome you are," Abadon finished answering all Roland's questions in his short concise backwards way of talking.

Roland supressed a shiver. Yep, gross!

Reaching the exit, they stepped out onto an airport sized ledge and Roland's mouth dropped open at the panoramic view spread out before him.

Abadon glanced down and couldn't resist, "swally," he said softly, and gave a short chuckle when Roland's mouth snapped shut immediately in response.

"Where are we?" Roland breathed. His eyes didn't know where to look, there was so much to see. The view from the top of the mountain was like nothing he had ever seen before. Steps led downward and a spraying, sparkling waterfall cascaded over them, sending droplets of water onto Roland's dark hair. It wasn't the steps or the water that amazed him though, it was what lay beyond that truly took his breath away!

A vast land spread out before his eyes, colors stretched as he viewed it through the clear falling water. Giant orange colored trees with large wide trunks filled a huge forest. A multitude of green, yellow and pink colored plants, flowers and shrubs covered the ground. Most astonishing and spectacular of all was the hundreds, maybe thousands of castles spread out as far as the eye could see. Castles like in Scotland and England.

Wow! Holy crap! Unbelievable! It was a city of castles.

Leaning forward slightly, Roland looked down squinting at three castles that even from this height, stood out from the rest. Not only were they the largest of all, with huge sweeping turrets, multiple levels, round towers, walkways and open courtyards with flowers and water features, they were the only three that weren't covered in browns, greys, reds and greens.

One was located at the top of a plateau overlooking the city. This castle was completely white, from its walls to its gates and even the rooftops. At the base of the hill and slightly off to the right, was a second exceptionally large castle that was the most amazing solid blue color. The color was the same swimming pool blue color that he noticed come from Abadon's white markings whenever he used his magic. And the third, at the base of the hill, but slightly off to the left, was built completely with shining black stone.

"That is so the jam! Who lives down there in those ginormous castles?" Roland spoke in hushed tones.

"Strange words you have. Soon enough see you will."

Ha, he had strange words? The guy was a regular comedian.

"Took you two long enough. Did you stop for tea?" Sir Balkan's unexpected voice made Roland jump three feet in the air.

Stepping away from the side of the open doorway, he didn't continue, because his attention was elsewhere, his eyes on the sky, a small smile lit his face. Quiet for a moment, he finally turned to Roland and said, "hold onto your shorts kid, you are about to meet Eltanin."

"Who's Eltanin?"

"My master," Abadon answered, bowing.

Confused, Roland stared at Abadon, then at Sir Balkan who was bowing as well.

Gusts of wind sent Roland stepping backward and swooshing sounds had him raising his hand to shield his eyes against the glare of the sun. An immense shadow blocked out the sun and the view below, hovering outside of the water curtain.

"Holy crap, what is that?" Roland cried. "Is it another gargoyle?" Panic started to set in. Oh no, not again! He wasn't waiting for the attack to start this time. He did what any thirteen year old boy would do, or so he told himself. He hid behind Abadon!

Pulling him out from behind his back, Abadon said, "Come Roland, meet my Master."

His eyes boggled out of his head when the shadow landed on the ledge and a magnificent blue dragon stepped through the flowing water.

A deep rustic voice boomed out, "Welcome Roland White, to the Realm of Abraxas!"

Roland couldn't respond at first, his throat bobbing up and down like a buoy in the ocean as he tried several times to swallow. His mouth opened and closed like a fish out of water.

His voice, after several tries still came out breathless and weak. "Whoa! A dragon!" He gulped, feeling a blackness closing in on him.

"Hmmm," the voice rumbled. "Abadon? I believe he might need some assistance."

Abadon turned to Roland. Seeing the boy's white pasty face he instructed, "Drop head to knees."

Roland never even hesitated, but placed his hands on his thighs, bent from the waist and lowered his head as close to his knees as he could.

"Deep breaths take in and out, slow," Abadon said. "Better, yes?"

Roland stood up warily.

"Yeah, better I think," he responded as the blackness cleared away.

He stared hard at the dragon in front of him. "I, uh, I, well, this is impossible. I can't actually be looking at a real dragon, can I?" he finally blurted out.

"Not on your world, but here, in Abraxas, we are real and alive." The dragon responded with a small smile, his voice a soft, soothing, deep tenor.

"Not any dragon this be," Abadon interjected. "This is Eltanin, Guardian of the Realm! My Master," Abadon said with another low bow to the dragon. "Relieved I am to see you. Trouble we had. Very disturbing it was."

Roland wasn't sure what the proper protocol was in meeting an obviously important dragon, so he copied Abadon by

73

giving a low bow from the waist before rising up to say, "Uh, hello."

"You must have many questions Roland, but I wish to show you something first, I wish to show you our wonderful realm. Sir Balkan, would you assist the young one?" Turning to Roland he said with another smile, "We are going to take a ride."

Roland stared uncomprehendingly as the dragon lowered himself down on all fours. He was huge, his body larger than a school bus, with thick muscular legs and a long tail. There were no scales, but rather sky blue feathers that shifted and flowed like silk with every movement. Four silver curved horns, two on each side sat just above his ears. More feathers filled his massive chest and flowed down his legs to stop before scaled, clawed feet. Great feathered wings rested along his body and elongated feathers flowed down the tail.

Sir Balkan strode to Roland, grasping his elbow. "Put your foot on his leg. I'll give you a push and you can climb up onto his back."

"What? What? Uh no, that's okay, really, uh Sir Dragon, I don't need a ride. I'm okay right here." Roland stumbled over his words, his hands waving as panic raced through his body.

"You'll be fine kid. Come on, you've come this far. Not everyone gets to ride a dragon, and especially a ride on the Guardian. It's a great privilege, so buck up boy and get on," Sir Balkan said, hoisting Roland into the air until his foot rested on the dragon's bent leg. Letting go, Roland had no choice but to grab onto feathers to prevent himself from falling backwards. Looking up at the gigantic body, he was about to turn around and go back down, but Sir Balkan was one step ahead and gave Roland a big heaving shove. Rising up, Roland quickly snagged more feathers and was now hanging off the side of the dragon. Rather than stay hanging there, he slipped and slid as he climbed awkwardly up the side of the dragon's shoulder. He ended up at the base of the dragon's neck where he lay panting for a second, before lifting his leg over and plunked himself down, squirming around, trying to find a spot where he didn't feel like he was going to slide off. Finally feeling somewhat secure, he was breathing heavy from a mixture of exertion and a scared excitement.

"Hold on young one, and I will show you our home!" Eltanin said with pride. Roland felt muscles rippling beneath his legs, and leaning forward in panic, grabbed a handful of feathers as immense blue wings unfurled. The great dragon rose up into the air with smooth, level strokes of his vast wings and in seconds, they were airborne.

Roland wrapped his arms around Eltanin's neck as best he could, feeling more secure this way than holding a handful of feathers, and hung on for dear life. A great sweeping turn had Roland screaming first in fear and then in exhilaration. He wanted to sit up and throw his hands in the air, but the long plunge to the earth kept him rigid, every muscle tense and locked.

Around Abraxas they flew. Over hills, valleys, lakes, mountains and woodland forests. He saw tiny bodies below and when Eltanin swept low to the ground, Roland saw hundreds of toucan bird heads perched on bodies very much like that of a giraffe. Large colorful beaks squawked as their long necks bobbed up and down. Rising up, they crested a mountain top before skimming the rock as Eltanin dove straight down its sheer, rocky side.

Flying over a small body of water, Eltanin sent ripples racing outward with a slight gentle touch of his wings. Leaning over carefully, Roland looked down and saw mermaids and mermen swimming below the surface. Noticing the large shadow above, they flipped over onto their backs, coming up out of the water, waving and calling to them in squeaky, high pitched voices. Eltanin dropped his wing tips a bit more, sending water spraying up into the air like a water skier. Cheers and clapping followed them.

Leaving the water, Roland wiped droplets off his face with one hand, as they soared up into soft fluffy clouds. There, beyond the clouds, Roland gawked in wonder at a herd of white, winged horses playing tag with a green and white butterfly the size of an ostrich. When the horses saw the great dragon, they flew around him excitedly and then followed along, throwing their heads back, their manes streaming behind, neighing happily.

The boy and the dragon joined them in a game of hide and seek in the clouds, before dropping down to head for a large forest. The canopy was a multitude of colored leaves, blocking everything underneath from sight. As they dropped even lower, Eltanin gave a great flap of his wings and the multi-colored leaves flew up into the air. They weren't leaves at all, but tree sprites. Looking behind, Roland watched as they landed on the back of the dragon, almost completely covering him. He looked like a giant ball of rainbow colored cotton candy. The sprites chittered and chattered while they stared at Roland. One gathered up enough courage to fly over and land on Roland's shoulder. With tiny little hands, it touched his face. Looking back at all the others, it stuck its teeny tongue out at them and blew a raspberry. Roland burst out laughing which scared it away. Another took its place, followed by another and another, and pretty soon, Roland's head, hands, arms and shoulders were covered with the small creatures. They were all touching him, exploring his skin and hair. It felt like hundreds of ants were crawling on him and he had to fight the desire to shake them off.

In moments, however, the sprites flew off like a flock of birds when Eltanin dipped down suddenly. Roland could see a darkness looming ahead and they turned back before entering the strange barren, gloomy area. Eltanin informed Roland it was the Kingdom of Rallag. It was where the black dragon Rahm was hiding. The unnatural coldness of the air penetrated Roland's clothes and caused a sharp chill. A shiver rolled up his spine, and Roland was happy when Eltanin turned around to fly in another direction, away from the unpleasant, creepy feelings it stirred.

Roland watched in amazement as the yellow sun in the sky dropped away and a blue one took its place. He was stunned when he looked down and saw the blue rays didn't change the colors of the scenery below but only seemed to make everything brighter and clearer. He wondered when the next sun would come up and what color it would be. He knew there was five of them, remembering the scenes shown to him when Abadon touched his head.

The dragon soared over a multitude of villages that dotted the landscape, each one home to strange, wonderful creatures. One village boasted homes made of mud and straw, and had green ogres shaking fists and clubs at them until they seemed to recognize who it was and waves followed instead. Flying into a valley, shiny stones stacked in pyramid shapes housed tall, elegant elves, who never looked up, but continued about their business. Another village had goblins, another oversized birds living in incredibly large treetop homes covered in purple and pink leaves.

There was so much to see, so much to take in, it was overwhelming, and it didn't stop there. Next, Roland saw herds of incredibly strange looking creatures roaming below, carefree and unconcerned. Among them, a group of black and white striped elephants with four trunks; orange gorilla looking animals that were fishing on a river bank; hippos that were wearing dresses and floppy hats or pants, shirts and cowboy hats and were busy decorating their wet, gooey mud homes with round burgundy fruit and flowery vines; fat, lazy looking yellow blobs filled a pond, sprawled in the blue water like whales sunning on a beach, while bulging stomachs sprayed water in the air like a blowhole. One rose up out of the water, and Roland saw a round, bubbled head, large floppy ears, a piggish snout and small yellow eyes. Squinting, the eyes followed their progress above.

"What are those things down there in the pond?" Roland yelled over the noise of the wind.

"Polydoros. Lazy and harmless. They filter the algae from the water. This keeps the pond clean, allowing others to safely drink it. They are very useful."

As their journey continued, the blue sun eventually fell from the sky, and a green one rose, travelling up quickly, before stopping, held motionless in the sky. Remembering the moving pictures Abadon had put in his head, Roland realized there were two more suns to come. A pink one and a black one, which means it was probably afternoon.

Passing the base of a steep canyon, they disturbed cave dwelling griffins who rose up to join the flight. Roland thought they were really cool, with their eagle heads and lion bodies, until one got too close and nipped at his shoulder with its sharp pointed beak. Leaning sideways in response to the quick bite, it just missed taking a chunk out of his shoulder.

Eltanin twisted his head to the side and gave a warning roar. The griffins apparently got the message because they immediately scattered.

Eltanin made a wide sweeping turn and after flying quietly for a time, Roland could see the city of castles in the distance. The landscape around the city was vast, surrounded by clumps of huge forests, a large sparkling lake filled the horizon to the east and two rivers wound around towering mountains in the west. He could also see the shadow of a wall that seemed to go on forever. Roland could see no end to it, nor a beginning. He wondered what it was and what it was for. Was it keeping something out or keeping something in?

Directly above the city now, Roland could see wide cobblestone streets, stone walkways and wooden bridges joining everything together. Trees and flowering bushes filled empty spaces and he could see hundreds of colorful rooftops of smaller houses interspersed throughout, tucked in beside and behind the multitude of castles.

"What is that?" Roland leaned over, spying a large dust cloud racing toward the courtyard of the blue castle.

"Trouble," the dragon replied softly before resuming his flight downward, heading for the same courtyard.

6

The Centaur King

Landing in the courtyard, Roland crawled awkwardly, like a crab, off the dragon's back, resting on the bent foreleg before carefully sliding down the rest of the way.

The dust cloud swirled into the open castle gate, obscuring everything from view.

Coughing, Roland waited until the air cleared and saw a large group of.... No, it couldn't be! Rubbing his eyes, he looked again. Yep, it was real, or rather, they were real. It was centaurs, half horse, half human, a large group of them huddled together in the center of the yard. Their horse bodies were filthy with dirt and blood, and they were sweaty and shaking. One, the largest, stood at the front of the group, bowing low when Eltanin approached.

He was older, visible wrinkles and crinkles flowed out from the corners of his eyes and deep grooves followed down along his mouth. A long flowing white beard filled his lower jaw and chin, joined by a thick white bushy mustache, white eyebrows and white flowing hair. His human body was tanned a deep dark brown and the whiteness of his tail stood out in stark contrast to his equine body that was completely coated in a long, thick, silky, midnight black coat of thick horse hair. Leather ties circled his biceps and a pack of arrows hung from a leather pouch on his back. A thick wooden bow, painted and inset with jewels, hung suspended from his right hand. A glittering purple amethyst shone from the middle of the centaur's forehead, while sitting above it was a crown of branches encrusted with purple and green precious gems. Black armor protected his chest and shoulders, shimmering with purple, green and silver. He looked very regal, like a king, Roland thought.

"Master Guardian," the centaur began, "we were attacked on the western shore of Holiman Lake. The gargoyles ambushed us from the trees." His impressively muscular arms were covered in scratches, one really nasty cut still dripping blood down his arm.

"We will talk after your herd has been looked after, Tartae. Let us take care of your wounded and get them settled with food and drink." Raising his voice, Eltanin said, "Come, Centaurs of Overon. You are safe here. Let us assist you."

Just then, tall, thin elves along with short, squat goblins, poured out of the castle and began herding the centaurs inside. The centaurs followed in silence. Crying and wailing, with buckets of tears, would have been better than the silence and air of defeat that filled the courtyard.

"What of the rest of the herd? Are they safe?" Eltanin asked the one named Tartae, as they stood together watching the herd walk away with shoulders slumped, some limping, some hobbling awkwardly and still others with the slow weary steps of complete exhaustion.

"The main herd is safe at home." Tartae replied wearily. His wide muscular shoulders slumped in defeat. "We had gone on our annual Sponsorship of the Yearlings. There are still some unaccounted for from the attack though. They are missing, wounded, taken hostage or dead. It was completely unexpected and we were sadly unprepared. Rahm is no longer hiding his intentions. He is attacking and now no one is safe! What are we going to do about this?" The centaur demanded loudly.

"We will talk more soon. You have wounds that need to be attended to. Right now, I shall send Sir Balkan to retrieve any wounded and the dead as well as send a message to the kingdoms to be on alert."

Roland did not hear the reply because the conversation faded as they strode away. He couldn't help but notice the young centaur who had stood silently beside, but slightly behind, the one called Tartae.   He too had a gem in the middle of his forehead, but his was a bright lime green color, sending out green flashes every time his head moved. He had only a single green beaded chain around his neck.   Muscular, but much smaller, he looked similar enough to the older one, he could be his son. He too was tanned and his horse body a deep black, but his hair and tail were black rather than white, and his horse coat wasn't near as long as the other's. Roland couldn't help but stare. They were magnificent.

Roland wished he could help the centaurs somehow.   They looked so sad, so lost, so forlorn. He knew what that felt like, for he had felt it himself not all that long ago.

The pink sun replaced the green one as he stood uselessly in the courtyard, staring. He was stunned at the variety of color among the centaurs. Their upper human bodies looked just like any other person. They all had long flowing hair, but only the two black ones had the long coats on their bodies. The rest had short coats like the horses at home. There were palomino colors, browns, roans, reds, blacks, whites, paints and spotted appaloosas. All had lengthy, graceful, swishing tails that matched their hair color.

"Abadon, who was that and what is going on?" Roland asked, looking up at the warlock standing beside him.

"Rahm," he answered wearily. "Attacking he is. Stop him we must. King of Centaurs, Tartae is. Friends of dragons they are. Very bad this is." Waving over a young boy who was standing in the yard watching the herd slowly move away, so engrossed in observing he didn't see the gesture. "Stringley!" Abadon called impatiently. Turning toward the call, the boy limped across the courtyard with a scowl. Surprised, Roland realized it wasn't a boy at all, but a short, squat goblin.

Stopping in front of Abadon, the goblin did not look at either one of them, but glared at the ground. "Take Roland to the Avalon Room. Send food up." Abadon instructed.

"Yes Master Abadon," replied the goblin. He turned and stomped away, not looking to see if Roland followed.

Turning to Roland, Abadon gave a slight nod, "Night soon. Sleep. Meet again tomorrow we will." Abadon strode away with long purposeful strides.

"Abadon...." Roland called out, but the warlock did not stop.

Roland hadn't noticed until now how tired he was. Weariness seeped into every bone, his mind full of the wondrous things he saw and the dangers he had experienced, that he wanted nothing more than to have a break from it all, so he hurried to follow the unfriendly goblin before he got too far ahead.

Entering the castle, the goblin went down a maze of passages and before Roland knew it, he was completely lost. The beauty of the castle had his head swivelling, and at times walking backwards, trying to take it all in while still hurrying after the goblin. Roland walked with his mouth hanging open, glimpsing beautiful painted scenes on the walls and ceiling, marble figurines posed in alcoves, sculptures of mystical creatures stood guard, elaborate pillars filled cavernous rooms, statues, armor and weapons had places of honor along the hallways, plush wood furniture of all sizes issued invitations to come in and sit before the roaring fires, stained glass windows threw colorful rays onto floors and walls and thick hand woven rugs covered cold floors. It was as though he had entered another realm inside the castle. It was amazing, lit with candles and torches, like a castle from a Disney fairy tale.

The goblin stopped at a large wooden door. Swinging it open, he stood aside and Roland entered, then jumped when the goblin slammed the door shut behind him. Roland muttered to the closed door, "It was nice talking with you too!" Sheesh, what was that dude's problem? He needed a personality adjustment, check that, he needed a personality period!

Looking around the room, Roland sighed when he saw an oversized couch with a blue feather blanket and pillow.

Moments later, a small girl with long silver hair dragging on the floor, shyly brought a heaping plate of food into his room. He ate every bit of the strange but delicious food, then snuggled under the blanket and fell into a restless slumber.

The centaur king paced in Eltanin's colossal sized study. "Why have you summoned me here in secret Eltanin? And what is being done about Rahm?"

Sighing heavily, the dragon lay gracefully on the floor. "Secrets have become of utmost importance. Sir Balkan believes we may have a traitor in our midst. Rest assured, I am looking into this very carefully. Now, you are familiar with the Prophecy of the Spirit Dragons'?" At Tartae's quick nod, he continued, "We found the one from the Prophecy, the one to save the realm."

"I don't understand? Who is this chosen one from the Prophecy?" Tartae frowned. "Why don't you call the kingdoms together? Let us march to war on Rahm!" Tartae smashed a fist on his open palm.

Eltanin looked to the ceiling, saying a silent prayer for patience, as the centaur began pacing around the study. The centaur king was a great, noble creature, but he was also one who liked to lead and not follow.

"Abadon has foreseen that should we do this, march to war as you suggest, we will lose. None of us has the power and magic we need to defeat Rahm. It is too close to the alignment. Magic in the realm is at its lowest before a new alignment Tartae, this you know. How do you think Rahm and his gargoyle army can be defeated without powerful magic on our side? We have only one choice and one chance. Deciphering the Prophecy was our only hope." He avoided telling Tartae about the Timekeeper being stolen. That must be kept secret for now or the realm would plunge into panic and chaos.

Tartae stomped his feet, agitated. Striding to the window, he pulled the curtain aside and stared out at a perfectly manicured flower garden. Eltanin left him to his thoughts, staying still and quiet.

Tartae finally lowered his head. Sighing heavily, he turned back to Eltanin. Crossing his arms, he stretched the multitude of stitches on his arms and chest almost to the point of splitting open. "Then my son and I shall assist."

Giving a regal nod, Eltanin rose up gracefully, towering over the centaur. "You do not have to do this Tartae."

"Yes Eltanin, I do. My oath is to protect my herd at all costs. Today, Rahm brought the battle to the centaurs. Many innocents across the realm will continue to die unless he is defeated before the alignment. If this prophecy is the realm's only hope and only chance, it is not going to be done without us."

The dragon nodded his head in acknowledgement.

"You have not said the name of the one from the prophecy. Do not think I don't know you have not yet told me who this savior of the realm is. Well, keep your secrets for now, but I expect to know soon. What is the plan?"

"A small group must find and retrieve six powerful artifacts. They are key to the one from the prophecy defeating Rahm. A small group has a better chance of avoiding Rahm's watchful eye. It will be a dangerous undertaking, and the most important quest in the history of Abraxas."

Frowning, Tartae nodded slowly. "My son and I will make preparations for this quest."

"When do we leave?" The centaur king asked quietly, stroking his long beard.

"You will leave tomorrow evening. Does that give you enough time to prepare?"

"Yes, that will be fine." The centaur confirmed.

The figure hovering outside the closed door hurried away. Now was not the time to be caught eavesdropping.

7

The Talking Tapestry

Roland opened his eyes and stretched. Plucking at the large blue feathered cover, he felt like a giant bird was laying on top of him. Sneezing from a feather tickling his nose, he sat up to take stock of his surroundings as he had been too tired last night to pay much attention.

Floor to ceiling windows with open drapes let in a soft blue light. Holy crap! It must be close to noon. It made him think right away of his mother, and how she would have been pestering him to get up long before. This only made him feel sad though, so he got up, folded the blanket as best he could, even though it still looked like a big messy lump, and walked toward a humungous fireplace, rubbing his hands together. A roaring fire was blazing away, taking the chill out of the stone walls. The warmth soon eased some of Roland's nerves.

Across the fireplace was floor to ceiling windows, while another wall of the square room was full of blankets with pictures and paintings hanging on it. The last wall was completely filled with large leather bound books. Turning from the fire, he took a few hesitant steps to the books when he stopped in his tracks. He just realized something. There was no door! Where the heck was the door? They came in through a door last night. He remembered Stringley opening it and then slamming it once Roland entered. But where in the blazes was it now? It was like it had disappeared. How was he gonna get out of here? Maybe Stingley hid him in here and would tell everyone he ran away and he would starve to death and.....

Stop it, he told himself. He was letting his imagination run away with him. Think Roland think! Pacing back and forth, back and forth, circling the room, he examined the floor where a door might have left marks from being opened and closed.   Nothing! Zip! Zilch! Nada!

He sighed in frustration.   Running his hands through his hair leaving behind a spiky hairdo, he noticed a long, brown leather coat draped over a couch in the corner. Walking over, he touched the soft, supple leather. Deciding to try it on, he was pleasantly surprised to find it fit perfectly. Examining it closely, he found a multitude of pockets inside.   Some were big, some medium, some small and some so small he almost didn't find them. All he could fit in those ones was a finger. What good was that?

Leaving the coat on, he did a third tour of the room with no success in locating a door, when a thought struck him.   Smacking himself in the forehead with the palm of his hand, he couldn't believe he had been such a dope. The door must be behind one of those blankets hanging on the wall.   He didn't know they were called tapestries, handwoven with incredible detail, each one telling a story, preserving history for all time. To him they were hanging blankets, and one of them must be hiding the exit.

Approaching one of the blankets, he stared at the picture. It was of several knights on horses, decked out in lavish shining armor, standing in the centre of an arena. Townspeople filled the stands all around, watching, cheering and waving different colored flags. The blanket beside had a countryside scene with a castle in the background. A long line of knights riding enormous, powerful looking war horses with swords drawn with faces fierce and battle ready. They were travelling away from the castle down a worn bumpy road.

Stepping back, he looked at other hanging blankets and recognized a medieval theme. An extremely large blanket depicted a castle with knights riding in a courtyard full of cheering peasants. Roland didn't know if they were arriving in the courtyard, or leaving it. Another showed a royal wedding, and still another the coronation of a king. The colors, the weaving and the incredible attention to detail, gave the blankets a 3D look, like he could be looking out a window and watching each scene unfold below.

Come on Roland, focus, he told himself. He turned his attention back to the largest blanket and slowly pulled it back to reveal.... Well nothing, nothing but more stone! He was positive the door would be behind it, and was very disappointed he was wrong. There was no handle, no hinges, no nothing. Letting it fall back into place, he heard strange noises, like the fluttering of birds and whispering voices.

Frowning, he looked around the room. Empty. Well that was weird.

"Okay, that's okay," he spoke out loud, "I think we're on the right track. There has to be a hidden door. I just need to keep looking."

He lifted the next blanket to search behind it when an angry voice said, "I request that you watch where you are putting your hands!"

Roland froze for a moment, then whirled around in fear. The blanket fell back into place with a slight smacking sound when it flapped against the stone wall. "Who said that? Who's there?"

"Ouch,"

"Hey watch it!"

"Kindly remove your hand from my helmet."

"Can you not have your horse breath in my face?"

"Unless you want my lance where the sun doesn't shine on your person, you will remove your foot from my nose!"

The comments flooded the room. The voices were annoyed and angry. In the background, Roland could hear the whinnying and neighing of horses.

He whirled around and around, searching the room for the voices, but could see no one.

"You there, boy! Are you the one that has caused this spectacle?" The rest of the voices went silent when the commanding voice spoke.

Another voice piped up, "Easy Regar, he is just a boy after all. No harm has been done."

Roland whirled around again, still seeing no one. "Who's there? Who's talking? Where are you?"

A chuckle followed his questions. "Who I am, young one, is Sir Lancelot, and the where is right behind you!"

Roland turned quickly, his eyebrows drawing together in a frown of confusion. Biting his bottom lip, he saw nothing but an empty room.

"I still don't know where you are," Roland said, unsure if the voice was friend or foe or even worse....a ghost....or even worse yet, a whole bunch of ghosts!

"No reason to get upset lad. You are looking right at me!"

Wringing his hands, Roland squinted, thinking if they were ghosts, they would be invisible. He couldn't see anything but the blanket he had just lifted. And then he yelped and scrambled backwards when one of the horses on the blanket started to move. Holy crap! It was galloping. Right at him!

One of the knights on a large black horse rode towards Roland. As it drew closer, its size grew and when it reached Roland, the horse and rider were full size, so close and so real Roland could smell the horse's bad breath, and yet it was still on the blanket! How could that be?

The horse lowered its head, its nostrils even with Roland's nose and gave a great snort causing Roland's hair to blow backwards. Roland frowned. Did the horse just do that on purpose? The horse, as though knowing Roland's thoughts, nodded its large head and expelled a great breath of stinky air again right in Roland's face. Wrinkling up his nose, Roland barely restrained himself from waving his hand in front of his face. It could be worse he decided, the horse could be farting instead!

Turning the black war horse sideways, the knight removed his helmet, shaking out thick wavy black hair. With a quizzical look, he stared down at Roland.

"And who is it you might be?" the knight asked.

"I, uhm, I'm Roland. Are you r-really Sir Lancelot? Sir Lancelot of Camelot a-and King Arthur and the Knights of the Round Table?" Excitement and nervousness causing Roland to stutter a bit. This was incredible!

"I am he. Now why are you moving our home around with no regard for the chaos you are causing us?"

Roland didn't know for a moment what he was talking about but then realized he must mean the blanket. They were living inside the blanket, or were alive behind the blanket, or well, something. Trying to figure it out was hurting his brain.

"I am sorry sir, I didn't know you were in there." Roland glimpsed faces of the people peeking around the large horse, trying to hear the conversation, but hesitant to be too close. "I, uh, well, am new here and uh, well, sorry to everyone," he finished awkwardly. The massive horse pawed at the grass, and Roland wanted that nasty horse to stay right where it was. He hoped it couldn't step right out of the blanket and into the room.

"I was looking for a door, but I can't find it! I thought it was behind, uh, where you live. That's why I was moving it. Do you uh, happen to know where the door is so I can get out of here?"

But Sir Lancelot did not get a chance to answer. Nor did anyone else, because just then, Abadon appeared beside Roland, sending him three feet in the air.

"How the heck did you do that? I mean, how did you get in here?" Roland asked, relieved to know he wasn't going to be left in here forever. And then excitement filled him and he couldn't contain himself, "Guess what?" he said, hopping from one foot to the other. "Do you know the pictures there on the wall, uhm, on the material, those blanket things," he said, waving at the wall, "that they are alive, I mean the people on them…"

"Good day Sir Lancelot," Abadon said with a respectful nod to the knight, smirking at Roland. "Yes Roland, know I do."

Turning back to the knight on the horse, Abadon asked, "Camelot is well?"

"Ahhh, a fine day to you Sir Abadon. Good of you to ask. Camelot is very well. King Arthur has called a jousting tournament in honor of the return of his best and most favored knight. You have heard Sir Galahad returned? I have not seen him yet. I have missed my friend these many years. The kingdom buzzes with the news. Others talk of nothing but the Prophecy of the Spirit Dragons' and how it is upon us. They said

Eltanin searches for the one who will save the realm. Have you..," the knight stopped talking and slowly turned his head to look down at Roland. His eyes widened.

Before he could say anymore, Abadon raised his hand and shook his head no.

Shifting in his saddle, Sir Lancelot quirked his lips in understanding and said, "I hope that you will be able to join us at the tournament Sir Abadon. Mayhap you will bring your young friend with you?"

"Mayhap," answered Abadon. "Must go now. Quiet this visit I ask you to keep."

The knight nodded his head.

Seeming assured by this, Abadon turned to Roland, who stood wide eyed while trying to follow the conversation. He was pretty sure a part of that was about him. Something nagged at the back of his mind. He felt like he missed something really important, but couldn't quite put it together.

"Come Roland, go now we must. Eltanin wishes to show you something."

Heading for the fireplace, Abadon walked straight through the flames and through the blackened stone behind, disappearing from view.

Roland was unable to move a muscle. Abadon's head popped back through the flickering flames and Roland jumped. "Come. Quickly now."

"You want me to go through there?" Roland asked, pointing at the flames, but Abadon was already gone again and only silence answered him. Hesitating, Roland walked to the fireplace. He needed to test it out, not trusting he wouldn't burst into flames. He put the toes of his moccasins in the flame, holding it there, waiting. Nothing happened. It didn't catch fire. In fact, it felt like warm water. He stepped in with his hands extended out, unconsciously closing his eyes and holding his breath. Taking two more unbalanced, shaky steps, he opened his eyes slowly to see he had passed through the flames and was now facing soot covered stones.   Feeling with his fingers, he was astounded when they passed right through the stones.   Whoa!   Way cool!   Quickly moving through the wall, he emerged out the other side and smack…oof!   He ran into the back of Abadon!

Reaching behind, Abadon pulled him in front by his arm. "Tape you to back of me I should," Abadon muttered.

"Sorry," Roland mumbled back as they turned and headed down the hallway, "but you are used to all this magic stuff and I'm not.   You gotta cut me some slack here," Roland said, trailing behind, wondering what crazy unbelievable thing was going to happen   to   him   next.

8

Veil of the Spirit Realm

Following Abadon along the labyrinth of hallways, down multiple sets of stairs and traversing right and left turns, they finally came to a long stretch of corridor, where Eltanin patiently waited at the end of it. Behind the dragon, Roland could just make out two hefty blue and silver wood framed doors that rose up behind the dragon's massive frame.

Returning the Guardian's cordial greeting, Roland wondered what he was doing here. Before he could ask, the blue dragon spoke.

"These doors you see behind me Roland, connect our realm to the spirit realm. I know you must have many questions as much has happened to you in a very short time, however, if you are patient for just a moment, you will receive some of those answers that you seek."

"Okay, but how....?"

Abadon held up his hand and Roland fell silent.

"You see Roland, Abraxas is a very ancient realm, one of nine and is comprised of twelve kingdoms. Right now, you are in Katori, city of the dragons, in the Dragon Kingdom of Dragayo. Did you know dragons come in many colors, and have their own magical power? This makes us special as other beings in this realm rely on the magic released by the suns at the time of the alignment for their survival. Now, there are three dragon colors reserved for the three most powerful dragons of the realm. The Caretaker is white, the Guardian, myself, is blue, and the Protector is black. Together, we are the Keepers of the Realm. Before one of us perishes, another is chosen, as there must always be three Keepers. Since we live for a very long time

Roland, there has not been many. In fact, there has only been four sets of Keepers in the ancient line."

Shifting his large body, he continued, "Behind these doors, spirits of dragons from days gone by reside. Many centuries ago, they revealed a prophecy to us, the Keepers. It is destined to come true during one of the alignments. This prophecy is why you were attacked by the gargoyles and why you were brought here, to Abraxas. That is all I shall say for now. There is more for you to learn behind these doors."

Nodding to Abadon, Eltanin stepped aside and the warlock stepped forward. Raising his arms while speaking softly, blue magic flowed out of his white markings and he passed his hands slowly over two silver, plate sized inserts on each door. Throwing his arms up in the air, the volume of his chanting grew louder and goosebumps rose along Roland's neck and down his back. Slowly lowering his arms, Abadon's voice diminished before ending in silence. Taking a step back, the warlock stood still and waited.

The silver circles began clicking clockwise six times, before reversing their direction and clicking three more times. A heavy mist emerged from the space under the doors, crawling up the wood like a ghostly army, until the doors were completely obscured. Roland glanced at Abadon, who remained silent and still, watching, waiting. Roland instinctively took a step back. The mist hovered over the doors before rolling back down to disappear underneath, as though responding to an unheard command. The doors remained closed, but the silver plates now each contained a carved blue dragon laying on its surface. They resembled Eltanin, only in miniature. Their tails were wrapped around their bodies, their noses almost touching, eyes closed as though sleeping.

To Roland's astonishment, the two miniature dragons simultaneously lifted their heads, stretching and blinking blue eyelids, fringed by long lashes, and white sightless eyes roamed the hallway. Roland sucked in a sharp breath. They were blind! Identical down to every last tiny detail, their movements a mirror image of the other, their blue feathers glittered as though sprinkled with fairy dust. Swishing their tails back and forth, they spoke, the two voices blending together, one high and one low, melding together in a beautiful harmony of words. "Who wishes to open the veil and enter the Spirit Realm?"

Abadon answered with a slight bow of his head. "It is Eltanin, Guardian of the Realm. Wish he does, for boy, Roland White, to enter."

Their heads swivelled and unseeing eyes locked eerily on Roland, before shifting to Eltanin. Bowing their heads, they addressed the dragon. "Welcome Master. What is the spirit word?"

This time Eltanin responded and Roland gaped in wonder. Something truly amazing happened when the dragon spoke. Warm, soothing vibrations penetrated every single pore of Roland's body with the sound of the wind, the rain, rushing water and rolling thunder all at the same time. It was the most incredible thing. He heard it, not with his ears, but with his body, with his mind and with his heart. It was so beautiful, he wanted to shout with exhilaration and dance with delight. He felt so carefree and happy. Every trouble, every worry, every fret was gone.

"Whoa, that was so awesome!" he whispered reverently when the sounds faded away.

Abadon turned with a slight smile, knowing the moment was magical. Very few were ever fortunate enough to hear it, to experience it. "Ancient language of the dragons you heard."

"Sweet," Roland breathed. There were truly no words in his vocabulary to describe how incredible that had been.

"Welcome. May the magic of the realm be upon you," the twin dragons stated harmoniously, bowing their heads once more as the large doors slowly and silently swung open.

9

The Spirits

Leaning forward against the doorway, Roland peaked his head in, expecting to see something really awesome but disappointment filled him when he saw nothing except a thick, heavy white mist. Stepping back, he raised his head, the question in his eyes. What now?

Understanding the unspoken question, Eltanin looked down at Roland. "You may enter when ready."

"Me?" he squeaked. "You guys are coming in too right?"

"No Roland, this is for you only."

"I don't want to go in there by myself. What am I supposed to do in there? Why do I have to go myself?"

"The Spirit Dragons' have been waiting for you and you alone Roland. There is much you will learn in there. Listen very carefully to what they say. Listen with your head, hear their words with your heart and see their meaning with your mind," Eltanin said softly.

Roland felt hands on his back gently shoving him forward. Trying to twist around, he could see Abadon behind him. "Go now. Okay it will be," Abadon told him. Returning his gaze to the mist shrouded doorway, Roland felt one last shove that sent him stumbling awkwardly into the whiteness.

Turning in a circle, it was his turn to be blind. The doorway he just entered was completely obscured by the mist, and Roland was instantly lost, surrounded by the thick misty fog. There was nothing to see and nothing to hear. An uncomfortable silence, eerie and strange enveloped him. He rubbed at the rising hairs on his arms.

The mist began swirling gently as if disturbed by a breeze, a breeze that wasn't there, a breeze Roland did not feel. Leaning forward he watched and waited, but for what? He didn't know. Instinct told him something was in the mist. Something was coming.

Without warning, the mist blew apart and a shimmering, white, ghostly dragon soared through, circling Roland before he could so much as squeak. A long misty tail wrapped around him and a soothing warmth spread throughout his body, He felt mesmerized, almost hypnotized by the feeling. The dragon's tail released him slowly and the dragon floated in the air above him. Roland felt safe, his heart calling out to the spirit as if they were long lost family, reunited after centuries apart. Without thought, Roland reached out to touch it, but his hand passed through the haze, separating it for a moment before it returned to its previous shape. The dragon swirled around Roland one more time, before setting down in front of him, tucking its shimmering wings in before raising its head to sniff the air. Looking intently at Roland, it cocked its head from side to side like it was looking at a new, undiscovered species.

Roland stood like a statue, afraid to move and scare it away, afraid to speak and ruin the moment.

"You have crossed the veil and entered the Realm of the Spirit Dragons'. Are you the one we have waited for?" The dragon spoke so softly, Roland strained to hear.

Roland twisted his fingers together nervously. Was he? He didn't know. Was he supposed to answer, to say something? What should he say? His brain was incapable of forming a thought or a word. All he could do was stand and stare.

Walking around Roland, the white spirit sniffed and nuzzled the back of his head, neck and shoulders. Roland's heart beat faster at the contact, not in fear, but with a strange feeling of anticipation.

The dragon finished circling Roland, looking at him quizzically for a moment before the phantom eyes widened. Frowning intently, he raised his head, peering into the mist behind Roland. "What do you think Alcon?"

Not wanting to make any sudden moves, Roland turned his head slowly, looking over his shoulder. There he saw another ghostly, shadowy spirit dragon hovering behind him. This one was a soft blue color, just like Eltanin.

"Yes, he has come." Alcon responded as he flew leisurely over Roland's head. Roland followed the progress until the dragon hovered just above the white one. "Many years we have waited. The Prophecy is coming true," a rough, gravelly voice declared. "I have wondered when it would come to pass." Landing beside the white one, the blue dragon shoved his whispery muzzle into Roland's face. "Yes, he is the one. This you know Chelios. You feel your spirit in him, do you not?"

"I do," Chelios acknowledged. "But can he fulfill the Prophecy? Can he defeat Rahm? Can he stop the evil that threatens the realm?"

A third voice, melodious, velvety smooth and definitely female, joined the conversation. Disembodied, it floated around them. "Many trials ahead for this one who is so young, but his heart is pure, and I sense a greatness." A black spirit emerged from the fog to land on the other side of Chelios.

"Yes, a great courage he holds deep within him. A courage he does not yet know he possesses."

Looking from one to the other to the other, Roland felt insignificant among these three great, noble spirits.

"Uhm, sorry if I sound really dumb, but who exactly are you?"

The white one spoke first. "I am Chelios, prior Caretaker of the Realm. The new Caretaker is Chara."

"I am Alcon, former Guardian of the Realm. I chose Eltanin to take up the heavy burden and great responsibility of my duties upon my death."

"And I am Damone," the black spirit spoke, "Protector of the Realm. I chose Rahm as the fourth Keeper upon leaving the realm. Rahm," she said with sadness, "ah, Rahm, wish I do, for the power to change that decision now, for his heart went dark and cold. I chose him to follow me, for at one time he had a great love for all the creatures in the realm. Once, his heart was full of gentleness and kindness, but that is no longer." Her head fell as though too heavy to hold up and the wispy black dragon's eye filled with a single sparkling tear. Roland watched it gather in the corner before rolling slowly down her face. It hung suspended from her jaw like a dewdrop on a flower before finally letting go. Roland tracked the progress of the tear until it was lost from sight in the soupy mist that surrounded their feet. A single, sweet bell chimed when it hit the floor. His eyes continued to search for it, but it had vanished.

Chelios broke Roland's fascination with the tear. "It is not your fault Damone. We chose who would take our place based on the purity of their heart. There was none more pure than Rahm's. It is not for you to answer for his choices, but his."

"A relief it is to hear that Chelios, but no matter, my heart breaks for the realm, and I must carry the burden, for I alone chose him."

"Enough Damone. There is still hope. There is the boy!" Alcon's rough voice broke through the heavy curtain of sadness.

Looking up, Roland saw the ghostly spectres turn in unison and three sets of eyes scrutinized him, each silently weighing his worthiness. He shifted uncomfortably, feeling like a bug pinned under a microscope.

Chelios spoke to his fellow spirits. "He has many trials to face on this journey, this quest, but I do not see him doing this alone. I see three, no four companions by his side."

"Yes, yes," said Damone. "Worthy companions they are. One is branded a traitor, the one called Kentor. A hard road that one walks."

"Hmmmm, yes, much I see in Kentor. Much greatness and much destruction. Which will he choose?" Alcon questioned no one in particular.

Roland's head swiveled from one dragon to the next, trying to keep up with the conversation, but they spoke in riddles. Who was Kentor? If he was a traitor, why would he join Roland on this quest? Who else was going with him? His head swam.

"Uhm, excuse me uh, Great Ones, but why exactly am I here? Why would a prophecy talk about me? I don't understand." Roland said nervously.

Damone spoke, looking blindly into the thick mist above Roland's head, concentration heavy on her face. "The black dragon, Rahm, has turned against his vow of protection and has stolen the Timekeeper. He believes he can harness its magic, but only the Caretaker yields the power to release the pure magic of the universe in such a way as to last for the next five thousand years. The alignment of the suns is one month away. Rahm will not succeed in harnessing the magic and if the Timekeeper is not returned to the white dragon Chara, it will run unchecked throughout the realm with. The result would be the end of the realm."

Damone looked sadly at Chelios before looking away. Silence reigned for endless minutes before Damone's gaze returned to Roland. "It will be up to you to right the wrongs being done to our realm."

Roland gulped, putting his hands up on the top of his head, interlocking his fingers. "But why me? I don't understand! I don't live here, I don't even belong here. I don't know what is going on! None of this makes any sense to me." He dragged his hands down his face.

Alcon spoke in his gravelly voice. "Ahhh, but you do belong here Roland White."

"What? What do you mean?"

Chelios whispered something softly. Meeting Roland's gaze, he said mysteriously, "Watch Roland White, and learn."

The dragons' stepped aside, revealing the coiling writhing mist behind them. Roland watched as it formed into a solid, opaque glass. Cracking appeared on the glass, spidery threads that spread quickly outward like it had been hit with something heavy, before shattering into a million pieces. Roland instinctively turned away, protecting his face with his arm, but not a piece touched him, as the glass vanished in the air. What remained was an incredibly long mirror. Staring, Roland scrutinized the reflection of the lost looking boy standing, shrouded by a background of mist, isolated and alone.

Leaning forward, he waited for something to happen, but the reflection remained, and he saw what he always saw in a mirror. A slim form with dark brown hair that curled up on the ends, blue eyes, square jaw and a small, narrow nose. Glancing over his shoulder, he could see the three dragons situated behind him, wispy and silent, but when he returned his gaze to the mirror, he stood solo.

He waited. Just when he was about to turn and ask the dragons if he was supposed to do something, a flutter in the mirror caught his eye. What was that? It was his own reflection, first wavering then flickering, and then he was gone, replaced by something else. A picture? No, not a picture, a scene.

The mirror was showing Roland bodies of knights, hundreds of them, laying strewn about like dirty clothes. Movement caught his eye and he honed in on a large white dragon, feathers quivering, standing amidst the bodies, facing a tall, thin figure dressed in black. The figure was bent over, skeletal hands twisting and twirling something between white, bony fingers. A microscopic red glow began to form, growing larger and larger, as the hands continued to form it like molding clay. Even observing through a mirror, Roland could feel the evil pouring out of the black figure, as real and thick and substantial as he himself was.

Knowing a fatal showdown was about to happen, Roland's attention turned to the white dragon, feeling confident it would beat the bad guy. But his heart plummeted, when he realized why the feathers were quivering. It had been badly injured, blood appearing from numerous wounds, running unchecked over the pure white feathers, creating a sickly looking pink color. It shook with exhaustion, obviously weak and in pain.

Something shifted, the movement catching Roland's eye. One of the bodies, a knight, was slowly rising up off the ground. Standing, he swayed like a branch in a hurricane before taking stumbling, tentative steps in the direction of the dragon.

The red glowing object the figure held was now the size of a basketball. Red sparks shot out in all directions like a firecracker going off too soon. The mysterious figure cradled it between both hands before sending the red ball like a missile, straight at the dragon. Roland sucked in his breath. Oh no! He was about to witness the death of this great, magical creature. He wanted to turn his head away, his mind screaming at him "don't watch, don't watch," but he was powerless to even squeeze his eyes shut.

Just before the glowing fireball could smash into the dragon's chest, a body flew out of nowhere, taking the hit instead. The force of the impact sent it careening sideways, before spinning wildly, uncontrollably into a freefall toward the earth. Just before smashing onto the hard, blood soaked ground, the white dragon caught the lifeless body in its scaly palm, gently and reverently laying it on the ground. Roland could see the body was that of the knight who, just moments before, had risen slowly and painfully from the battlefield.

The powerful, turbulent flaming ball was deflected by the knight's metal armor, hurtling back toward the black figure, striking it in the chest. The figure was immediately engulfed in strange red and white sparking flames, screams of pain sounded in the stillness as it writhed and slapped, trying to put the flames out. But the exercise was fruitless, and the flames continued to burn. When they finally dissipated, all that remained was a pool of black, bubbling liquid. Roland felt queasy, his stomach rolling at the horrendous sight.

The white dragon stood over the quiet, inert body of the knight laying below him, his sides heaving, the blood still running. Hesitating for only a moment before lowering its great head, the dragon blew a gentle, velvety breath over the knight. A small, white, wispy, dragon form floated out of the dragon's mouth. Flying gracefully around the dragon's head, it reached out to tenderly touch the giant beast, before gradually floating down to hover over the face of the knight. Raising its ethereal head, it gazed at the white dragon one last time before turning swiftly and diving down directly into the heart of the knight. And it was gone!

The knight took a momentous, wheezing gulp of air before sitting up, drawing in more oxygen, interspersed with raspy coughing.

The scene began fading and the mirror once again showed only Roland's reflection. Staring, he watched as the solidity of his form diminished little by little, turning him into a ghostly caricature of his real self, until nothing remained in the mirror but the mist behind him, and then it to dissipated until the mirror was gone, leaving only the thick whiteness of before.

"I was the white dragon you saw," said Chelios, "and the knight who gave his life to protect mine was your ancestor."

Roland turned.

"It was I who restored life to the knight. I willingly separated a part of my spirit and bestowed it upon him as a gift in return for his sacrifice. My spirit has been passed to all the firstborn of his generations since. The powerful magic contained in my spirit has been waiting many centuries to reawaken, to be used by one who is worthy of its power. The time has come Roland. Your ancestor was from Abraxas, and you have this realm in your blood. You also have my spirit, my magic. You are a part of me. This is why you have been chosen to save the realm and why the prophecy speaks of you. Only you can use my magic to defeat Rahm."

"But how do I do that?"

Staring at him for a moment, the white spirit dragon swished his ghostly tail and blinked large, wispy eyes. "As you just witnessed, only a great sacrifice will stir my dragon spirit."

"You mean," he gulped, "I have t-to die?" he stuttered.

Roland's question was met with silence.

Chelios looked deeply into Roland's eyes. "You are the only one who has the power to defeat Rahm. I cannot tell you how to use the magic of my spirit, but I can tell you it is there, in your heart and in your soul and if you prove worthy, it will save your life!"

"So I don't have to die?" Roland asked quickly.

Again, he received no answer. Alcon rose up on his hind legs, wings spread wide. "It is time. We must go now." Looking down from his great height he said, before turning and disappearing into the mist, "Trust in yourself!"

"Wait," Roland cried out, "don't leave me yet. I need to know more!"

Damone came next, swirling around Roland, before whispering in his ear, "Believe in the magic and where it came from!" Her movements were graceful, silent and delicate. She too, parted the mist, and disappeared into its thickness.

Turning to the remaining spirit, Roland stared at Chelios. "Please," he pleaded, "stay. Don't go. You must tell me more. How do I defeat Rahm? How do I use your magic? How can I save the realm? What do I need to do?"

Rising into the air, Chelios's wispy wings gently disturbed the mist with each slow deliberate flap, until it was hard to discern the spirit body from the mist. From his lofty height, he spoke one last time, "Trust in my spirit Roland, for it is your spirit too." And with a sudden single twist of his body, he was gone.

Turning in a circle, mystified and bewildered, Roland wondered if he would ever understand everything they told him, and more importantly, if he would ever see them again. He felt empty and drained after their departure, like they took a piece of his soul with them. He wished more than anything, that they would come back.

10

Spiff

Roland found himself back in front of Eltanin and Abadon with no recollection of how he had gotten there. The large wooden doors were closing behind him, shutting out the realm beyond, securing the spirits on the other side. He wanted to shout, "No, leave them open, they might come back," but no words would form on his lips.

A flick of Abadon's wrist brought forth a small glass jar full of purple liquid.

"Drink this," instructed Abadon as he handed it over to Roland. "Refresh you it will."

Roland only continued to stare blankly, his mind still in the fog, in the spirit realm, replaying the words of the dragons'.

Abadon gently took Roland's hand in his own, wrapping it around the jar and raising it to his lips. Instinct helped Roland swallow the liquid, feeling the cool freshness of it travel down his throat. Abadon lowered it, waiting until Roland returned. The faraway look in his eyes wilted away, his body shuddered and trembled before he gave his head a slight shake. He wiped his mouth with the back of his hand. When Abadon gave control of the jar to Roland, he quickly took another drink.

Roland sighed. The drink revitalized him and he felt much better. It looked a lot like purple Kool-Aid, but tasted like watermelon and strawberries. Deciding if a sip did a little, a lot would do more, so throwing his head back, he noisily guzzled it all down.

Handing the empty jar to Abadon, he didn't see it magically disappear because his attention had already been redirected. Something was poking sharply into his other hand. It was clenched into a fist, gripping something inside. Raising it up, he tentatively opened one finger at a time, revealing a beautiful teardrop shaped crystal, the size of a plum, lying in his palm. Brilliant facets of color burst out in all directions like a diamond in the sun.

Picking it up between his thumb and forefinger, he examined it more closely, turning it first one way, then another. "What is it?" he asked.

"A gift." Eltanin's eyebrows rose in surprise when he saw what Roland was holding. "A great gift!"

"From who?"

"That is a dragon tear. You must guard it very carefully. Tell me Roland, which of the Great Ones shed a tear?"

"It was, uhm, Damone? Yeah, the black dragon Damone. Whoa, it is soooo cool. What do I do with it?"

"For now you will put it somewhere safe. It is very precious. Do not speak of it with anyone. Many out there would do anything

to have that tear. Keep it secret, Roland."
Thinking for a moment as he stared at
Roland's hand holding the treasure, he gave
one last instruction. "I believe Damone
wished for you to keep it with you."

"Yeah okay." He slid it into one of the
many inside pockets of his coat. Patting the
pocket reassuringly, he turned his attention
back to Eltanin. Being given that tear by
Damone had instilled a confidence in Roland
he had not felt since this whole ordeal
started. He felt, in a peculiar way, this was a
sign that they not only believed in him, but
would be with him no matter what
happened. Rubbing his hands together he
said boldly, "Alright, what's next?"

Abadon masked his surprise at this
seemingly new and confident boy in front of
him. Glancing at Eltanin, Abadon spotted a
thin, pale figure rounding the corner at the
end of the hall. Frowning, he beckoned the
figure to them. Seeing the motion, it hurried

toward them with an awkward side to side gait.

Reaching them, it bowed to Eltanin. Turning its body to Abadon, its eyes searched and found Roland. Staring at the boy unabashedly, Roland stared right back. He was looking at an owl with large eyes, flat face and hawk-like beak. The circle of feathers around each eye made them seem incredibly large. A subtle mix of browns and whites on the feathers surrounding the head gave the impression it was very austere and wise. Its body however, was something else. It was a twig split at the bottom creating two legs, and two leafy pieces stuck out sideways as arms. It looked completely ridiculous, like a thin branch with an owl head stuck on top which was exactly what it was and Roland fought back a giggle. Its height was just slightly taller than Roland, and its round head bobbled precariously on the top of the thin twig.

"Yes Master Abadon," it enquired, its beak clacking as it spoke, not breaking eye contact with Roland.

"Spiff! Abadon said fiercely, finally getting the stick owl's attention. "Playing with magic again you have been?" Abadon sternly looked the owl up and down, a frown appeared between his eyes, and his mouth turned down. Uh oh, thought Roland, someone was in big trouble.

"Sorry Master." Spiff answered quietly, swivelling his head around on the twig shoulders so that he was facing the other way, like he was embarrassed to be seen like this.

Roland stared at the back of the owl's head, completely confused.

"Told you I have, all lessons stopped. Magic must be preserved. Not enough in realm to play. Stop you must!" Abadon's voice was really angry. "Fix yourself you will," Abadon commanded, "then show Roland Katori. Ensure food he gets."

"Yes Master, oh yes, yes. I can do that," Spiff said excitedly while rotating his head back to face forward. Turning to Roland, Spiff clapped his twiggy hands together, causing leaves to cascade down to the floor. Abadon snapped his fingers to get Spiff's attention, "Make sure safe he is!"

"For sure Master. I will take very good care of him. You can trust me Master."

Only Roland saw Abadon roll his eyes before grasping Roland's upper arm to lead him a few steps away. Speaking quietly, he said, "Tell no one where you came from or why. Say only visiting city, you are. Be careful what say to Spiff. Not good at..." trying to find the right word, Abadon made a zipping motion on his lips with his fingers instead. "Understand?"

Roland nodded his head grinning. "Yeah, you mean he doesn't know how to keep his mouth shut."

"Yes, shut mouth. Good. Go with Spiff. Show you around he will. Have some fun.

Meet again later. Take you to your parents then, I will."

"Okay, yeah, that would be great!" Roland exclaimed, feeling lighter, happier at that news. He knew they were still stone statues, but he needed and wanted desperately to see them.

Returning to Spiff, he and Roland turned and started down the long hallway.

"And Spiff," Abadon called out, "No more magic!"

"Yes master," Spiff replied quickly, turning his head and body sideways as he continued walking. "I won't, I promise," he said in a sing song voice, giving a slight wave of a leafy arm.

Reaching the end of the hall, they turned left, out of sight of Eltanin and Abadon. Spiff immediately slumped against the wall.

"Whew," he said wiping a twig across his forehead, then looking at it with a scowl. "Well, that went well, don't yah think. Oh, I guess I better fix this before we go any further, or I will be in real deep droppings if Master sees me still like this later. Okay, cross your fingers. I sure hope this works better than last time." Closing his eyes he put his head back against the stone. His twig arms started waving around while strange words click clacked out of his beak.

"Hey man, what are you doing?" Roland stepped back in alarm putting his hands up defensively.

A poof and a flash surrounded Spiff, and Roland was now looking at a full-fledged owl. Standing eye to eye with Roland, the twigs were gone, replaced by wings and a round, feathered body with thin clawed feet peeking out the bottom of the feathers. Yellow eyes blinked at Roland, before a wide, beaky smile appeared.

"I'm me again! Welcome back Spiff!" he said to himself, twirling around before patting his wings over his body, making sure everything was there and in the right place.

Jumping in the air, he clicked his feet together happily.

"I wasn't sure if it would work. Just before being a twig, I had horns, hooves and a tail. I even scared myself," he said laughing.

"How long have you been a twig?"

"Oh, since last night," he said, with a flick of his wing as though it was no big deal.

Staring at the bizarre bird, Roland shifted, "How come you can do magic?"

"All Prefix owls can. Haven't you met any before?"

"Uh, no," Roland replied, Abadon's warning still ringing in his ears. He couldn't tell him he came from another world, a world where owls were a lot smaller, didn't talk, and couldn't do magic.

"Oh, well that's too bad. Where do you wanna go first? We can explore the whole wonderful City of Katori," he said spinning around happily. "Obviously you haven't been here before, otherwise I wouldn't be showing you around. What kingdom do you come from?"

Roland needed to quickly change the subject so that he didn't have to answer. Thinking fast on his feet, he ignored Spiff's question to ask his own. "Why did Abadon give you the gears about using magic?"

"Give me the gears? I don't understand. You have strange speech. You must be from Zontari. I heard Zontarians speak with strange words."

Giving a slight nod, Roland let him think he had guessed right. "About the magic thing?" Roland tried to steer him back.

"Oh yes, well, we are coming up to the Festival of the Suns, you know. That's when they align, the suns that is, but everyone knows about the Festival so ignore my rambling. Anyway, since it is only a month away, magic in the realm is at its weakest and Abadon insists that we use it very sparingly so that there is enough to get us thru. Some however," he leaned down to whisper to

151

Roland like they were co-conspirators, "have been saying there is even less than there should be, way less, but no one seems to know why. Some say, someone is stealing the magic right out of the Timekeeper!" He stated as though giving away the greatest secret of all time. He had no idea how close he really was to the truth, but Roland did. It was because the Timekeeper had been stolen.

"What else are they saying?" Roland whispered, playing along.

"Ooh, ooh," Spiff got excited, thrilled to be sharing all the gossip with someone eager to hear it. "They are also saying the dragons are giving their own magic to keep us all going until then. That is why Abadon is mad at me. No one is supposed to be using unnecessary magic because it is draining the dragons. But I don't believe that nonsense. Abadon is just being bossy. He likes to be bossy you know," Spiff informed Roland with a sniff, puffing out his chest and bobbing his head up and down, proud of being so smart.

Roland wanted to ask him more questions, keep him talking, but Spiff had already turned and was skipping down the hallway. Shaking his head, Roland couldn't help but smile. The stern professor look on the outside was completely at odds with his carefree, silly personality.

Definitely strange, thought Roland following, but a thousand times better than that mean grouchy Stringley. The thirteen year old boy in him quickly rose to the surface and with a whoop and fist pump, he jogged after the owl. Time to do some exploring, Roland style!

Abadon had waited until Roland and Spiff turned the corner before speaking quietly. "Very good it is Master Eltanin. The boy saw the Spirits. It is confirmed. He is the one."

"Yes Abadon. That is very good. King Tartae and his son will be joining you on this most important of quests. You know we must find the ancient artifacts if we are to succeed?"

"Yes Master. Has Chara devised a plan to reveal their hidden locations without causing a new war amongst those that possess them?"

"He is working on that. He must have a solution by this evening. Things are unfolding more rapidly than I expected. The gargoyles finding Roland on his earth world means they know who he is. Rahm wishes to use the boy's power, but if he cannot, he will destroy him in order to stop him. This quest will be very dangerous Abadon, and the magic continues to drain rapidly. I feel it. My own magic is depleting at an alarming rate more and more every day." He sighed. "Very difficult it is to put the fate of all magical creatures and beings of our world in the hands of a boy. However, we must put faith in the Spirit Dragons' for they continue to guide and protect our realm."

"Much to prepare Master. Get ready I will. Leave tonight we do." Bowing low, Abadon strode away quickly, while the dragon walked more slowly, deep in thought.

Roland quickly caught up to the owl and Spiff immediately began chattering away about the goings on in the castle. Like how the tree elves were fighting with the water elves because the tree elves were bragging their flower gardens were way nicer than the water elves' ponds. He talked about the goblins complaining about Stringley, who was the head goblin and how grouchy he has been lately. And he told Roland about how the Abatwa had been causing all kinds of conundrums because they were shooting their poison arrows at everyone without asking their question first.

"Who are the Abatwa, and what question are they supposed to ask first?" Roland asked intrigued.

"Wow, you really are a Zontarian huh? Well, the Abatwa are tiny humans. I mean, soooo tiny they can hide under a blade of grass. Most roam around the realm, but a group of them made their home here in the castle about ten years ago. The first time you meet one, it will ask you "From where did you first see me?" Now this is the tricky part, because if you answer wrong, they will shoot you with their poisonous arrows. It won't kill you because it is so teeny, but it sure stings and can cause massive swelling which takes forever to go away. You will get this question each time you meet a new one."

"So, once you have met them all, they won't ask you anymore?" At Spiff's nod, Roland narrowed his eyes and asked suspiciously, "Have you been shot before?"

"Yeah," Spiff answered, obviously embarrassed.

"How many times?"

"Oh just a couple." He waved his wing evasively.

156

"How many is a couple?" Roland persisted.

"Twelve." Spiff sighed.

"Twelve! How come so many?"

"Well, because I always forget the answer," said Spiff. "It's really not my fault. They shouldn't be allowed in the castle with those arrows anyway. It's not like they are out in the wild anymore you know." He sputtered. It was obviously a sore point with the owl.

"Well, just in case I meet one, what is the answer?"

"Ah, yes, the answer, hmmm, well..."

"You don't remember again do you?" Roland surmised, throwing up his hands.

"Yes, yes I do, just give me a second. Ah yes," he said snapping his wing tips together like Roland would snap his fingers. "The answer must be this," looking to make sure he had Roland's full attention, "you must say you saw them from a treetop!" He said proudly.

"What? That doesn't make any sense. How could anyone see someone that tiny from a treetop?" Roland said in disbelief.

"Ah," Spiff waved a long finger-feather in Roland's face. "But that is the key. You see, they are incredibly sensitive about their size, so if you say you saw them from a great distance, like a treetop or a mountaintop or something like that, you have just given them a great compliment and...." He paused for effect, "they won't shoot you," Spiff finished with a flourish.

"Oh, and one more thing," Spiff said as though remembering something important.

"What?"

"If you ever step on one, it is a death sentence!"

This had Roland looking around the floor hastily for teeny tiny human people. Spiff started hooting in laughter. "Don't worry Roland, my new friend," he said smacking Roland on the shoulder, "you won't step on any right now. They only come out at night."

Relieved, Roland had one more question about the Abatwa. "If they are so touchy and possibly dangerous, why does Eltanin let them stay in the castle?"

"You my friend, are very smart. That is a very good question. You see, they are incredibly talented carvers, embroiderers, painters and stone masons. Every tapestry in the castle, every carving, whether it be stone or wood, have all been designed and created by the Abatwa. They have a magical ability, and if every stone block in this hallway was to fall down right now, by morning it would not only be fixed, but incredible scenes would be carved into it as well. They are amazing artists. I am sure you have seen some of their tapestry work. They hang all over the castle." Lifting an eyebrow in question, Roland had to tell him he didn't know what a tapestry was. When it was explained to him, he didn't tell Spiff he thought they were blankets. He found out the tapestries came to life because of the Abatwa's magical ability. That explained Sir Lancelot!

Reaching a large foyer, guards on either side of enormous doors opened them, revealing a cloudless green sun filled day. Spiff and Roland emerged from the castle and started down the human sized steps built along the side of the enormous dragon sized center steps.

Rubbing his wings together, Spiff exclaimed, "This is going to be fun! Let's go to the market first."

Roland shrugged in agreement, following Spiff toward the cacophony of noise on the other side of the courtyard gates.

11

The Katori Market

Wondering around the market, Roland was bombarded with incredible sights and sounds. Many magical creatures were busy bartering and sampling the countless wonders spread out along the flagstone street. There was a huge assortment of food, none of which Roland recognized. The smells, strange and mysterious, yet tantalizing at the same time, caused his stomach to growl in response.

He saw stalls filled with silks, spices, satins, leathers, dishes, utensils, furniture, feathers, eccentric clothing and outlandish materials filled every available space in the market. Trinkets, jewels, gems, pendants, rings and jewelry of all kinds, hung from stands, sparkling and glittering as they danced and jingled from ribbons, beads, metal and string.

Roland's eyes burned because he was so afraid of missing something he kept forgetting to blink. Beautiful woodland elves walked in groups of two and three, pointing, giggling and trying on flowered hats. He watched as griffins took turns landing at a meat stall to squawk at a vendor, pull out one of their own feathers in trade for a piece of what looked like sausage, before flying away again.

Hooded figures in long dark robes, faces concealed, lurked about in gloomy corners, while knights spoke with blacksmiths, ordering new swords, armor, helmets and an assortment of hardware for their horses. Women in long elaborate dresses conversed in a strange language, while darkly tanned women, dressed like belly dancers, gracefully meandered, shopping for jewelry, flowers and material.

Merchants called out their wares boisterously, shouting loudly over the music of flutes and harps that filled the air. Owls, just like Spiff, called out greetings as they passed by, looking curiously at the boy beside him. The only way Roland could tell the difference between them all was the different hats they wore. Not a single one had the same, and each head piece was more outlandish than the other, like it was some kind of competition. One owl had a yellow hat as tall as he was and had shark sized teeth hanging all over it. Another was wearing a boot on his head with a flowering plant draping down out of the top. Every hat was completely ridiculous and bizarre.

"Spiff, why do the owls have funny looking hats on and why aren't you wearing one?"

"Well, you see," Spiff rubbed his wings over the crown of his head, "we all look so much the same that someone, a very long time ago, suggested we wear something that allows others to tell who we are. One of our wise elders suggested a colored tag on our leg. We tried that, but it was too hard to see, and everyone was still confused as to who they were talking to, so long story short, it ended up being hats. Aren't they beautiful?"

"Oh, yeah, absolutely gorgeous," Roland said sarcastically, but the owl either missed the nuance or chose to ignore it. "So owls wear those hats all the time?" At Spiff's nod, Roland shook his head, not understanding why anyone would want to wear one of those silly hats once, let along constantly.

"But why don't you wear one?"

"Oh I did, but one of my magical spells went, well, kinda wrong, and my hat ended up running away on me. I never did find it, and I can't seem to find that perfect new one. Choosing a hat is a very important, delicate process," Spiff said, puffing out his chest.

"Yes, I could see how it would be," Roland replied, chuckling to himself. He could have made some crazy suggestion, like a giant purple feathered banana, but decided to just keep it to himself. He was afraid Spiff may actually like idea and start walking around with one on his head.

Roland was startled when Spiff reached out and yanked him sideways. "Hey, what the heck?" Roland asked as Spiff let go and he fixed the crushed sleeve of his nice leather coat. Before Spiff could explain his strange behavior, Roland started bouncing up and down just before a ginormous foot stepped down right where they had been standing only seconds before. They had just narrowly been missed being flattened like pancakes by a giant, dirty, smelly foot. Everyone in the market was being violently jostled about as they scrambled to get out of the way.

Roland stepped back out onto the cobblestones to watch the giant's progress, his mouth hanging open until Spiff put a long feather under his chin to close it. Roland didn't even notice.

He was amazed that not one stall or person was squashed as the giant went on its way down the street. Wearing stained green shorts and a white, torn shirt, Roland could see bald patches littering the back of its big, round head, and it was filthy. Chunks of mud fell off its body with each ground shaking step, revealing more caked on mud underneath. It progressed along the street until it stopped at a stall at the far end of the market. There, it bent over and handed the shopkeeper three live red and green clucking chickens. Taking the hens, the shopkeeper went inside before returning a moment later, lugging a gargantuan long, black thing behind him.

"What the heck is that thing he's bringing out Spiff?" Roland asked, but Spiff only held up his index feather, indicating Roland should just wait and see. Puffing with exertion, the shopkeeper finally dropped it at the giant's feet. The giant picked it up, examined it then grunted his approval. He then wove it into the waistband of his tattered, dirty shorts. Roland couldn't believe it. It was a belt!

Roland shook his head in amazement as Spiff told him they could keep going. Resuming their wonderings, Roland saw beautiful witches, and ugly, creepy looking ones. He saw tall, elegant elves in fancy clothing, as well as short, squat dwarves who were equally well dressed, but more in armor and furs than the embroidered silks and satins the elves seemed to prefer. Small elephant looking animals ran around the market like dogs would at home, searching for scraps of food with short stunted trunks. They were black in color with white and yellow spots. Giant eagles paraded the cobblestones like royalty, interested in the gems and jewels as much, if not more, than the women were. Crocodile men in tuxedos and top hats promised potions for all types of maladies, while fortune telling parrots professed to tell of grand futures. Satyrs giggled and whispered amongst themselves, while Minotaurs trailed behind beautiful harpies like lovesick puppies. The harpies looked exactly like peacocks, only with stunningly beautiful female faces.

Dragons, smaller than Eltanin, bartered in the marketplace, filling the streets with all shades of color, except blue, white or black. Catching the eye of a red one, Roland quickly looked away, embarrassed to have been caught staring.

Spiff was busy pointing out creatures that bordered on the odd, while others were strangely peculiar, and the rest, well, the rest were just downright weird and wacky.

Roland's head was spinning and he finally asked Spiff if they could stop and get something to eat. He was starving!

Finding an empty table at a side cafe, Spiff told him to stay there while he went to get them some lunch. When he returned, he put a heaping plate of food in front of Roland with a flourish.

"I picked all my favorites. I hope you like it," Spiff said, joining Roland with his own full plate. Roland tucked in with gusto just as his stomach growled embarrassingly. What could he say? He was a growing boy!

He started with red pancakes that tasted like ham, before spooning up some purple rice that was like peanut butter and jam. He tried some small, flat, chunks of yellow tortilla type bread and round orange meatballs, whose flavor reminded Roland of eggs. Too hungry to talk, Roland just shovelled the food in, chewed, swallowed and repeated, until every speck of food on his plate was gone. Drinking some of the same purple juice Abadon had given him earlier, he wasn't as surprised this time by the big boost of energy it gave him. Spiff told him it was called hasper juice. This time it tasted like blackberries and honey. He felt much better now that his stomach was full and patting it contentedly, he sat back, feeling tired, He burped loudly, thumping his chest with his fist like his dad always used to do. Remembering his manners, he politely excused himself.

Spiff hooted delightedly, letting his own little belch out before rubbing his protruding stomach. "I am stuffed," he pronounced. "And you Roland, do you need more?"

Roland groaned. "I couldn't eat another bite. I am full to the top! That was off the charts Spiff, thanks man."

Spiff clapped in satisfaction. "I just love your strange language. Now, come along Roland, much more we have to see."

"Actually Spiff, do you think we could do more sightseeing later? I'm feeling kinda tired."

Spiff's face fell in disappointment. Roland quickly added, "I do want to see it all Spiff, really I do, and you have done such a top notch job already, showing me the market and stuff. It's been totally awesome, but I have had a really long morning and now that

I ate lunch, I just need a bit of a rest is all, you know?"

"Yes, yes Roland, of course, I will take you back to the castle. We can see more after you have rested. There is the Dragon Museum, Cyclops Bay, the Rainbow Ride, the Hill of Bones, the...." He stopped when Roland raised his hand.

"I get it Spiff, I get it. You pick the ones you like best, and we will see them later okay?"

"Oh, oh," Spiff hoped from one foot to the other, his wings flapping happily. "Hmmm, I will have to think about that. Let's see, ah yes, we absolutely have to go see....." Their voices faded away as they headed back to the castle.

A hooded figure stepped out from the shadows. It had been watching them closely, and now turned with a sweeping flourish of a long black robe, to glide away as silent and deadly as a viper.

12

The Wolven Wolf

As tired as Roland felt, he was unable to sleep, flip flopping from side to side on the oversized couch. Sighing in frustration, he couldn't stop visualizing all the foreign and exotic creatures he had seen at the market. It was so hard to wrap his head around it all. He wished his friends were here because they were never gonna believe him. His face fell. He was assuming he would get home someday to tell them about it. Maybe that would never happen.

Roland was jarred out of his thoughts when Stringley suddenly stepped through the flames of the fireplace and into the room.

Like last time, the goblin said not a word, only indicated with a slight wave of his hand that Roland should follow. Roland wanted to say something sarcastic to the goblin, but didn't. The truth was, the goblin kind of scared him, but he could still feel annoyed at Stringley's rudeness and he did.

Once again, Roland found himself in the maze of the hallway, the silence broken only by the clopping of the goblin's long, dirty black toenails on the stone floor. They finally halted in front of a large blue door.

"Aperi," Stringley said in a gravelly voice, and the door silently swung open to reveal a large office, full of books and a roaring fire. Abadon sat behind an oval blue desk, while Eltanin lay on the floor to the side. They were quietly conversing, not yet noticing the newcomers. Judging by the concerned looks and frowns on their faces as they spoke, it wasn't a good conversation. Roland didn't think he was gonna like this.

Bracing his shoulders, Roland started to step through the doorway, but just as he did so, Stringley grabbed his forearm in a grip of steel, squeezing painfully, crooked black nails digging deep. "You think you are going to save this realm little boy, but you're wrong. You will fail and you will die."

With that, the goblin shoved Roland's arm away like it was full of contagious warts. With one last snarl, Stringley turned and hobbled away. Roland rubbed his arm, thinking he should probably disinfect it now.

What an ugly little creature. Roland wondered why Eltanin put up with him. He contemplated whether or not he should say something about Stringley's nastiness, but decided he didn't want to come across as a tattle tale.

"Ah Roland. Come in, come in," said Eltanin. "Don't lurk in the doorway. I trust Spiff showed you some of our wonderful city?"

"Yes sir, it was incredible." But before he could fill them in on all the fantastical things he saw, Eltanin spoke again.

"Roland, please come and sit. I have something very important to discuss with you."

Walking to the desk, he plunked himself down in the chair across from Abadon.

"Roland, I wish we had more time. It is very unfortunate that we don't. You know you are the chosen one, the one to save our realm? In order to do this, you must go on a very dangerous mission, a quest if you will. Abadon, King Tartae and his son Pentally, as well as Sir Balkan, will be going with you. It has been decided that you will all be leaving tonight."

"Tonight? But, I can't leave tonight. Spiff was going to show me more of Katori. I only got to see the market. We were going to go to some museum and a bridge or bay and some bone pile or something, plus a whole bunch of other really cool things. I'm sorry, I just can't go tonight. Maybe tomorrow night?"

He nervously picked up a small, blue speckled egg off a small stand on Abadon's desk, tossing it up in the air and catching it. Just before tossing it again, Abadon leaned over the desk and took it away, giving him a *"don't touch anything"* look.

Roland rolled his eyes. Stretching, he started to get up, thinking he was successful in putting off this quest thing, but he was wrong.

"I am sorry Roland, but it has to be tonight. There is no time to waste. There is much you need to accomplish before you came face to face with Rahm."

"Yeah, okay, right," he said plopping back down in the chair. The truth was, he was terrified and it had been worth a try to use Spiff as an excuse to put his purpose here on hold for as long as possible. Too bad it didn't work. Nervously, he reached out, picking up another strange object off Abadon's desk, twirling it around in his fingers. It reminded him of a hot dog except it was a reddish orange color which is what stopped him from maybe taking a bite. He gave it a wave in the air at the same time as Abadon reached to take it away. Abadon was too late.

"Ugh," Roland cried, dropping it on the floor in surprise when a shower of red and orange sparks flew out one end. Spreading quickly, the sparks coalesced into a shape, a very large shape. A body, legs, head and muzzle formed, snarling and snapping at Roland. Roland tried to spring off his chair to escape the deadly, drooling mouth, but he fell awkwardly instead, rapidly crab crawling backwards in fright, until his body collided with Eltanin's chest. He could feel a deep rumbling vibration against his back.

"What-t is tha-at thing?" he stuttered, staring at a massive, burning flame of fur on a very, very big wolf-like creature. The red and orange striations of color made it seem as though there was a huge bonfire in the room. A bonfire that was baring long serrated fangs at him, while large amber eyes glared unblinking.

Abadon came around the desk, approaching the wolf with his hand out. "Good it is to see you Tazar. Mistake it was to call you. My apologies Great One." Abadon spoke quietly, reaching out to rub the head that was almost bigger than Roland. The wolf, after one last snarl at Roland, rubbed against Abadon's hand, plopping himself down on his haunches, putting his head level with Abadon's shoulder.

"Tazar is the last of the Wolven Clan. Abadon found him when he was a pup, saving him from certain death from the Griffins. You called him forth with the Wolven whistle you had in your hand. Abadon will send him back."

"You mean he lives in that hotdog?"

The rumbling resumed, shaking Roland up and down.

Understanding dawned on Roland. Twisting around, he looked up at the dragon. "Are you laughing?"

The rumbling grew stronger.

"You are! You're laughing at me." Roland wasn't sure if he should be relieved or insulted.

"Maybe a little." The dragon admitted, wiping a tear from his eye.

"Humph, or maybe a lot." Crawling out from under the dragon's chin, Roland stood up carefully, not wanting to draw the wolf's attention with any sudden moves.

Staring, he heard the words come out of his mouth before his brain could stop them. "Can I, uh, do you think I could pet him too?" What? What was wrong with him? Was he nuts? He didn't really want to get that close to it, did he?

Abadon gave Roland a severe look in reprimand, clearly not impressed with Roland's shenanigan. Roland hung his head, kicking at the rug covered floor with his foot. Softening, the warlock looked at Eltanin in exasperation. A slight nod from the dragon had Abadon sighing. "Come then, pet him if you must."

After getting a slight nudge from Eltanin's nose, Roland felt his feet moving closer and closer until he was standing in front of it. Abadon gave the wolf a reassuring pat on the head and Tazar then stretched out his neck to sniff at Roland's feet. Following his nose all the way up to Roland's forehead, he gave a snort.

"Awh, gross!" Roland said, wiping wolven spit from his face.

"Like you he does," Abadon said with a smirk.

"Yeah right. You probably told him to do that." muttered Roland, wiping his hands on his pants.

Reaching out, he carefully touched the top of the wolf's muzzle. When his hand remained attached to his arm, he stroked the fur slowly, hesitant and unsure. Getting braver, he rubbed faster until both hands were sunk deep in the luxurious, fiery fur coat. He scratched the wolf's neck and behind its ears until the wolf's tongue was hanging out in pure enjoyment. The wolf leaned into Roland's hands, obviously wanting more, while its tail thumped the floor.

"Enough. Return he must. Tazar, time to go it is."

"But I want to…"

Roland was cut off when the wolf turned a circle around Roland before giving him a lick with a sloppy pink tongue, leaving a trail of saliva from Roland's chin up to the top of his head. His bangs spiked straight up in the air from the impromptu hairstyle.

Abadon had retrieved the whistle off the floor and raising it to his lips, he gave a single blow. Roland didn't hear anything, but the wolf immediately raised its head and in an instant, ran full speed at Abadon, leaping as if going for Abadon's throat only to shatter like broken glass in midair. Red and white shards replaced the solid wolf form, turning into flaming streaks as it was sucked back into the whistle. Just like that, the Wolven wolf, Tazar, was gone.

"Will I get to see him again?" Roland asked hopefully.

"Another time. Listen you must. Done we are not."

Roland walked dejectedly to his chair, disappointment rolling off him in waves as he dragged his feet before dropping his butt back in the chair to hang his head.

Abadon returned to his desk, ignoring Roland's theatrics. He bent down to retrieve something from the floor. Picking it up and placing it on the desk, Roland looked at it from the corner of his eye, not wanting to show too much interest and ruin his "poor me" show. He saw it was a brown, unassuming, bland looking knapsack. Oh whoopy, an old bag. Not anywhere near as cool as the wolf.

"Open it," Abadon said to Roland.

Standing up, Roland pulled it towards him, looking first at Abadon, then at Eltanin, trying to feign indifference, but the slight widening of his eyes proved otherwise. What the heck could be in there? He hoped nothing was going to jump out at him. Untying the strings on the flap, he flung it back at the same time as he retreated. Nothing. Feeling foolish, he stepped forward and leaned over the bag. It was full of rolled up old papers.

"What are those?" he asked reaching in to pull one out.

"Do not open it here Roland, for it is not safe to do so. These are scrolls given to you by Chara, the white dragon. They are the most important thing you will be taking with you. You see Roland, many centuries ago, six kingdoms became embroiled in a nasty quarrel that almost came to war. Each kingdom created a secret artifact to use against the others. The artifacts have enough magical capability that they could destroy the entire realm. None of the kingdoms knew what the other crafted, or what power it had, but all were incredibly dangerous. Chara, our white dragon, realizing how far this dispute had gone, stepped in and mitigated peace.

However, something still had to be done about the artifacts. So Chara took the artifacts, mixed them up and returned one to each kingdom."

"Oh that is so smart," Roland jumped in snapping his fingers. "I get it. None of the kingdoms know how to use the artifact they got so they can't use them against each other, but they still have a powerful weapon if they ever need it. So they were all happy and war was avoided right?"

Giving a regal nod, Eltanin confirmed Roland's hypothesis. "Very good. You are correct. In order to defeat Rahm, you need those artifacts Roland. Chara had sworn an oath to all six kingdoms to never tell anyone anything he knew about the artifacts. Since that was many centuries ago, most around the realm have forgotten they even exist.

Only those kingdoms who have them remember, and not only treasure them above all else, but guard them heavily."

Pausing to let that all sink in, Eltanin continued, "Chara has devised a way to reveal the artifacts location and power to you without breaking his promise to them." He lifted the knapsack in one claw, letting it hang, three pairs of eyes moved side to side in tandem with its swinging motion. "The answers are in here. Written on these scrolls, are the clues you need to retrieve those artifacts."

Scratching his head, Roland asked, "Why can't we just go to the leaders of those kingdoms, tell them what is going on and how badly we need them. Wouldn't they want to help and just hand them over?"

"Simple this would be, but part with them they will not," Abadon said. "Unfortunate it is, but only one choice we have. Steal them we must!"

Plunking himself down in the chair, Roland threw himself backward, crossed his arms and looked up at the ceiling. "Man oh man, I knew I wasn't going to like this talk. It just keeps getting better and better. Is there anything else I need to know?" he asked grumpily.

"Do not despair Roland. You are not alone. I believe you can do this, you must believe also. Now, for better news. Abadon has figured out a way to return your parents to the living. However," he held up a paw, when Roland jumped up, "he cannot until this quest is over because it requires much magic to reverse the stone spell, and unfortunately, right now, there is not enough in the realm for him to do so. But rest assured, when this is over, it is the first thing he will do!"

Staring down at the floor for a moment, Roland realized it could be worse. At least now there was hope they wouldn't be spending all of eternity as stone statues.

"Now, I am sure you would like to see them before you leave. Spiff would like you to join him for supper and then Abadon will take you to your parents. When you are finished, it will be time to leave. Your associates on this quest will be assembling at the stables."

"Yes?" Eltanin inquired, seeing the boy had something on his mind.

"Can I ask you something, uh, in private?"

"Abadon, if you would excuse us?"

Abadon looked at Roland questioningly, but Roland refused to meet his gaze. Leaving the room, Eltanin waited until the door closed behind the warlock before asking, "What is it you would like to know?"

Chewing on his lip, he gathered up the courage to blurt out, "Well before I leave, I have been wondering something, and since I don't know if I will ever return, I, uh, well….." Roland's words faded away as he shifted in his chair, his face red.

Raising an eyebrow, Eltanin only waited patiently.

"Why do you have feathers? I always thought dragons were covered in scales."

"Ahhh that is a very good question Roland. I do believe you get that from dragon stories on your world. It is easier to show you than to answer Roland," Eltanin replied and with a whispered command, his feathers began moving, standing straight up in the air before morphing into large blue scales. Once changed, row by row they snapped into place with perfect soldier like precision. Layer by layer, the feathers transformed into iridescent blue, impenetrable armour plates. From the tip of his nose to the end of his long powerful tail, the massive dragon was now covered in scales. Roland could see white markings of swirls and symbols, glowing a soft blue, just like Abadon's. Not a single section was unmarked, from his face to his horns to his legs to his feet. It was a breathtaking sight.

"We call forth our armor only when it is required," Eltanin explained.

With that, he spread his great wings. The long feathers were gone, replaced with thick, narrow plates of glistening blue scales. The wings spanned the room like a Boeing 747, scored as well with those mysterious, mystical white markings. Rearing up on his hind legs, he gave his wings a small flap. It was enough to blow Roland's hair back and have him grabbing frantically at the arms of the chair before he was flipped over backward with the force of the gale.

"Whoa, that is the sweetest!" he breathed.

Acknowledging the compliment with a slight smile, Eltanin tucked his wings back in and the process reversed. From the tip of his tail to the tip of his nose, the scales, row by row, reverted back into the soft, blue silky feathers. To Roland, well, that was the greatest, coolest, sweetest, sickest thing he had ever seen and his mouth hung open in awe, respect and admiration.

Abadon returned through the door after knocking. Roland had been too focused on the dragon to hear him and jumped when Abadon, standing beside him, leaned over to whisper "swally" which sent Roland's mouth snapping shut like a triggered mousetrap. At Abadon's big grin, Roland rolled his eyes, "Oh ha-ha, very funny! Hey," he said, crossing his arms, "don't you know the meaning of the word private?"

Eltanin smiled at Roland's question to Abadon. "Rest assured Roland, Abadon does not know what you asked. He only just returned. It must be important if he interrupted us. Now come closer for I have one more thing to tell you."

Stepping close to the dragon, he leaned his head forward as Eltanin whispered in his ear. Nodding his understanding, he stepped back.

"Go now and join Spiff for something to eat."

Heading to the door, Roland stopped while reaching for the handle. Turning slowly he hesitantly asked, "Do you breathe fire too?"

"With magic I can, but the fire breathers live in another realm. They are very dangerous and very mean and therefore are not allowed in Abraxas."

"Oh, okay, good." Not knowing what else to say, he pulled open the heavy door with a grunt. He was surprised to see Spiff hopping up and down in the hallway with excitement.

Clapping his wings together, he said, "It's about time you came out of there! Come on, come on Roland lets go! We are having tantella, mustair, choco puffs, gazant and hasper juice for supper. You will love it. It is delicious."

Since Roland had no idea what any of that was, he rubbed his hands together and replied in exaggerated delight, "That's great Spiff! Those are all my favorites."

Walking away, Roland tuned Spiff out, who was extolling the virtues of warm mustair over cold. He was wondering why it felt like he was going to his last meal.

13

A Last Goodbye

Roland felt someone shaking his shoulder. "Sir, sir!" a voice persisted from somewhere far away. Groaning he lifted his head, his neck stiff and sore. Shoot! He had fallen asleep.

"Master Abadon said it is time for you to go to the stables. They are waiting for you there."

Roland rubbed his eyes, looking up at a young knight dressed in armor like Sir Balkan. A helmet covered his head, while one hand held a sword at the ready, the other a shield. The metal was all in the same blue and silver.

Looking over at his parents lying on the stone slab, he fought back tears. Rising to his feet slowly, he massaged the back of his neck trying to get the kinks out. Picking up the knapsack that had rested on the floor beside him, he flung it over his shoulder, adjusting his long leather coat.

Approaching his parents slowly, he stepped up on the ridge surrounding the slab and looked down at them sadly. "I have to go now Mom and Dad, but I will be back, I promise. And when I come back, Abadon is going to fix you. You won't be like this forever. Just hang in there a while longer, okay? I'll see you soon."

Turning, he saw the young knight positioned at the side of the door, his sword put away, although his hand remained on its handle. Meeting Roland's gaze, the knight gave him a slight nod. Nodding back, Roland left his parents in the hands of the knight.

Exiting the door, Roland saw two more knights stationed outside and felt like a huge weight just lifted off his shoulders. Eltanin was making sure they would be safe while he was gone by posting extra guards. Letting out a deep breath he hadn't realized he had been holding, he stood straighter and walked with purpose down the hall. Time to go kick some butt and save this realm!

Now, where the heck were the stables?

14

Invisible Ride

Spiff caught Roland in the courtyard, heading to the stables.

"I just heard Master Abadon is taking you on a tour of the realm. You are so lucky! I wish I could go along with you," Spiff said, his owl eyes looking sad.

"It's okay Spiff, I will be back before you know it. I have to be, you still have lots of stuff to show me here right?"

"Oh yes, oh yes, I do Roland, I do. I shall be very bored while you are gone." He announced dramatically, putting his wing to his chest, the other to his forehead, making Roland smile.

"I'll see you soon Spiff, I promise. Don't turn yourself into a chicken or anything while I'm gone okay? And watch out for the Abatwa's." Roland told him.

Hooting, Spiff walked away with a final wave of his wing.

Reaching the stables, Roland stopped in front of Abadon.

"Roland," Abadon said with a graceful nod of his head. "King Tartae, Centaur Clan of Overon," Abadon said indicating the large centaur, "son, Prince Pentally."

Roland turned to the two centaurs and said hello. The centaurs, clad in armor, wore long draping capes that flowed down their backs, along their horse body to end at their tails. The king's cape was black with a rich purple lining, the prince's a lime green. Bows peaked out over their shoulders and arrows hung at their hips, contained in leather pouches. They looked dangerous and ready for battle and Roland felt very intimidated by them.

Prince Pentally returned Roland's greeting quietly, but King Tartae turned to Abadon with astonishment on his face. "This, this boy," he sputtered, sweeping his arm at Roland, "is the one from the prophecy?"

"King Tartae," Abadon scowled, "voice keep down! From prophecy he is! Discuss later we will.

Tartae stomped his feet, agitated. He was obviously angry and wanted to say more, but chose to stay silent for the moment.

Sir Balkan stood gazing into the distance as though paying no attention whatsoever to what was going on around him. But Roland knew the knight didn't miss a thing.

Well, alright then, isn't this just going to be a blast, Roland thought to himself. Standing there, feeling very awkward and uncomfortable, Roland's eyes locked on the swishing of Prince Pentally's tail. Back and forth, back and forth it went, just like a pendulum on a clock. Roland thought the two centaurs were incredibly majestic and stately, even if the king was, well, the other word for donkey.

"Ready we are?" Abadon asked, looking to each one for confirmation. After receiving four head nods, he called out, "Ride!"

Here we go, thought Roland looking around expectantly. His eyebrows drew together. Okay, hmmm, strange. What exactly was it they were supposed to ride? They were the only ones standing there. He had assumed they would be riding horses because they were meeting at the stables, but there weren't any horses saddled and ready. He had to admit he was secretly relieved because he had never been on a horse in his life. They couldn't possibly be riding the centaurs, could they?

The centaurs, as if hearing his unspoken thoughts, bent over to retrieve bulging saddle bags laying at their feet, swinging them up and over their backs. Tucking the saddle bags beneath their long cloaks, they turned and headed off.

Just then, two young boys in blue pants and white shirts overlaid with black vests, ran by Roland to the stable doors. Each grabbed a handle, and with a great heave, swung them wide open. Standing with their heads bowed, Roland could hear the clopping of hooves, but couldn't see anything inside the darkness of the stable. Four additional stables in the courtyard shook and rattled as though some very large creatures were trying to get out.

Roland was thinking walking would be just fine with him, when the two boys started shutting the stable doors, lowering a wood beam across, locking them tight. Scratching his head, Roland was completely confused.

"Alivento!" Abadon shouted, giving his hands a clap.

Before Roland's eyes, three white, massive bulls appeared out of nowhere. His eyes goggled, his mouth dropped open, his heart stopped and sweat instantly popped out on his forehead. Shaking his head and crossing his arms, he knew there was no way that he was getting on one of those things! Nuh uh.

Not a chance, not happening... and why was everything so big here? He would have been happy with a Shetland pony or heck even a pogo stick, but these things? Really? No way!

Sir Balkan gave Roland a smack on the back of his shoulder as he walked by. "Come on sunshine, time to ride." Roland lurched forward with the force, but wasn't really paying attention as he was completely focused on Abadon who approached the largest of the three beasts. Standing in front of it, Roland heard him say, "Zantos, old friend. Good to see you it is." The bull gave a shake of his head, and Abadon, as quick and nimble as a rock climber, put his foot into some kind of saddle looking thingy and swung himself up and on.

Roland watched as Sir Balkan's bull lowered himself down on all fours, so the knight could reach the stirrups and then, he too was sitting atop a white beast.

Roland, as slow as a snail, walked to the last remaining bull. The bull looked down its nose at Roland and gave a snort. Roland jumped three feet in the air. The bull snorted again three times in a row. Roland had a funny feeling it was laughing at him!

Roland reached up to touch it, his arm stretched way over his head, when the bull gave a head shake. Roland almost filled his pants! He felt heat rise up his neck as Sir Balkan chuckled. "Come on kid, we don't have all night. Just get on!"

The bull, after one more single snort, sank down on all four legs. Roland was way too short to reach the stirrups, and after trying unsuccessfully a few times, landing once in the dirt on his butt, he looked at Sir Balkan.

"How exactly am I supposed to do this? I can't reach that foot thing to get on."

"Climb up his front leg." Sir Balkan call back, as his bull started walking away.

Maybe he could do it like he did when he got on Eltanin. And so, climbing up the bull's foreleg, he stretched his leg across to the stirrup, swung his other leg around and he was on. He did it!

Shifting around, he tried to get comfortable in the weird saddle, which was made more difficult because the bull started walking as soon as his butt landed on the saddle. He slid side to side, trying to find some kind of leverage to hold him in place. He really didn't want to fall, it was way too far down.

Deep indents were set forward toward the top of the shoulders of the bull. This made some sense to Roland because the beast was so wide, there was no way that it could be straddled like a horse. Shoving his feet awkwardly into the holes, he leaned backward into the tall, rounded back of the saddle. That was better. He felt much more secure.

Looking at Abadon, who was just in front of him, he noticed that his saddle had raised sides on it. Reaching down carefully with his fingers, he felt panels on both sides. Lifting them up, they snapped into place. The panels not only created a partially square chair, they were also great armrests. It was actually quite comfortable and he sat back, trying to relax.

It wasn't long though before he began shifting around restlessly. The knapsack with the scrolls was digging into his back. He first removed his coat, and then slipped the sack off his shoulders and tucked it in beside him. Putting his coat back on, he patted the pocket with Damone's dragon tear to make sure it was still safe and sound. Yep, all good!

And so the quest begins, he thought as they passed under the crisscrossing metal castle gates and into the city of Katori.

15

A Pocket Full of Fire

The centaurs were already out of sight, heading through Katori at a gallop, while the other three moved at a slower pace. The size of the bulls made their progress slow as they had to ensure they didn't step on anything as they picked their way along the cobblestone paths.

Sitting forward on the back of the white bull, Roland was looking around, when he was surprised by a tiny yellow creature. It was the size of a small bird, with gossamer wings and thin, red, tail-like ribbons, and it was swirling in front of his face like a fly. Waving to shoo it off, it returned. Waving at it again, this time with both hands, a series of chirps and trills filled the air. Losing his balance, Roland fell backwards in the saddle, his legs flying up like a ridiculous yoga move. Sitting up, his face red, he looked around quickly to see if anyone had been watching. No one seemed to be paying attention.

"What the heck?" Roland said out loud, swatting at the pesky little bug again as it returned to fly around his face. He was trying to see exactly what it was, but it was too fast, zipping around his head and face in streaks of yellow and red.

"Not harm you. Fire sprite it be. Like you it does," Abadon said, not turning around in his saddle.

"Lucky you." Roland heard Sir Balkan mumble from up ahead.

"What does that mean?" Roland asked suspiciously, narrowing his eyes. "Why am I lucky it likes me?"

Sir Balkan turned sideways to look back at Roland. "They are a pest. If it gets into your pocket, you will never get rid of it. They are annoying and noisy, like having a pet mosquito." Sir Balkan smirked, as the little creature flew at Roland's chest and in the blink of an eye, crawled into the inside chest pocket of his jacket. "Look at that, too late,"

"What do I do Abadon? How do I get rid of it? Will it bite me?" Roland asked with a touch of panic.

"Hurt you it will not. Good sign it is."

"Why is it a good sign? Why don't you like them Sir Balkan?"

"I told you, they are annoying. And they start fires when they get mad. They can be very spiteful and mean. One once burnt a man in his bed when he was sleeping because he forgot to leave the window open for it."

That explained the name, Roland thought.

"Well, what do I do with it now?" Roland asked, afraid to move in case it started him on fire!

"Loyal they can be. Treat well and help you it will," Abadon responded, giving Sir Balkan a sharp look.

Sir Balkan only shrugged in response.

Looking down at his chest, Roland carefully pulled the jacket open. A teeny face stared up at him with great big, bright, green eyes. Blinking at him, it chittered away, as though telling him a whopping story. A small, round yellow head with a tuft of red hair sticking straight out on the top between pointy little ears and a little black nose, made Roland think of a miniature troll. A skinny yellow arm with three nubby fingers popped up and reached out to him. Deciding it was so ugly it was cute, he lifted his finger to it. It wrapped its arms around Roland's finger, rubbing its head on the pad like a cat. It started vibrating and the outside of his pocket started to turn yellow.

"Hey, he's not pooping in my pocket is he?" Roland asked, filled with both panic and disgust.

"No, glowing. Happy he is."

"Oh, okay I guess. But he's not going to poop in there right?" he asked Abadon, who only shrugged in response. Well that wasn't reassuring.

Removing his finger from the fire sprite's hold, Roland let his jacket fall back into place since he didn't know what else to do. The little sprite stopped vibrating and fell quiet for a moment, before Roland could feel moving and shifting against his chest. What the heck was it doing in there now? Slowly pulling open his jacket again, he was surprised when he didn't see its little head. It was gone! Where did it go? It had to still be in his pocket somewhere! Frowning, he carefully pulled the pocket open with his thumb and forefinger. Hoping it didn't bite him, he peered inside. Nope it was still there, all snuggled in a little ball at the bottom, the long red ribbons wrapped around it like a blanket.

Roland could see it was wearing red and yellow polka dot pants that were either too small or just too short as its yellow legs showed almost to the knees. Drawing its skinny legs up to its body, it tucked little hands under its cheek and closed its eyes. In seconds, Roland could hear it snoring softly. A small smile lit his face as he guided the jacket back against his chest carefully so as not to wake it up.

Turning his attention back to the ride, Roland was astounded to see the quiet street was now lined with dragons. Every open space was filled, and as they began passing by, Roland was stunned when the dragons began, one by one, to slowly bow their heads low and spread their wings out. Up in the sky, more dragons filled the air, taking turns to swoop down in front of them, bowing their heads as well.

"What are they doing Abadon?" Roland asked quietly.

"Respect to us they show. Bow to us they are. Very rare this is."

They were magnificent! It was incredibly humbling to see these magical beasts bowing to them and Roland felt a bolt of fear strike his chest. What if he failed them? He was just a boy and this, well, this was the most important job he had ever had. More than ever, he wished he was at home and that this had never happened.

He drew himself up, sitting straight on the white bull, trying very hard to look grown up and confident. He felt anything but that!

"Do they know what we are doing? I thought it was supposed to be a secret?" he whispered to Abadon frowning.

Abadon bowed his head regally in return to each dragon. He didn't answer Roland until the last dragon was behind them and they were out of the city. Only then did he address Roland's question, their bulls walking side by side.

"Dragons know dangerous quest we undertake. Know, also, only hope to save realm we are."

Roland tried to swallow, but the inside of his mouth had turned to cement. He knew this quest was going to be dangerous and the goodbye they just received from the dragons made Roland feel sad and anxious. This was a very big burden for a small boy to be carrying on his shoulders. Hanging his head, he tried desperately to think of another way to save the realm. He just didn't see any other way.

They all continued along in silence for a while, each lost in their own thoughts.

Roland couldn't bear the quiet any longer, it was too depressing.

"Why couldn't we see the bulls when they came out of the stable? Why aren't we just riding horses?" he asked breaking the silence.

Sir Balkan shifted in his saddle. Turning to Roland, he answered. "These big guys are Cretan bulls," he said reaching down and giving his bull a couple of affectionate pats on the side. "They are very gentle, loyal and intelligent animals. They are also very strong and very brave. We might need their help on this journey. They were invisible to our eyes because they have the ability to camouflage.

They can take on the landscape around them allowing them to blend in so well they are impossible to see."

"That is sick!" exclaimed Roland, "They are just like chameleon lizards that we have at home. They can do that too, but the bulls do it way better. I couldn't see them at all!" he exclaimed in wonder. "So how do they activate it, I mean, how exactly does it work?"

"They camouflage when they feel threatened or are unsure. When they came out of the stable, your scent, along with the centaurs, put them on alert. In defense they camouflaged themselves," Sir Balkan said with a shrug as though it was no big deal.

"Awesome." Another thought struck Roland. "Sir Balkan? Do you know Sir Lancelot?"

"I do."

"And do you know King Arthur too?" Roland asked excitedly.

"I do."

"Are you from Camelot? Have you done jousting tournaments? What is King Arthur like? Will I get to meet him someday? Why are you here and not there?"

"Whoa, slow down kid, you're gonna hurt yourself. Jeez you ask a lot of questions," the knight said shaking his head.

Abadon smirked, relieved someone else was getting them for a change.

"Let's see... yes to the first two questions, a great King and a great man, I don't know, and because I am the best, in answer to the last one.

"Oh, I see."

"Do you?"

"Nah, but I would really like to meet King Arthur someday. That would be so cool. Maybe he would even let me hold Excalibur! Do you think he would?"

Smiling, Sir Balkan just turned back around. Roland followed on his bull, chewing his bottom lip, envisioning holding the great sword and riding a big black war horse.

When the images faded away, he realized he had no idea where they were going.

"So, what exactly is our plan?" he asked Abadon.

"Search for first artifact we are."

"Eltanin told me not to read the first scroll until we reached something called Zamdruid Gate? I think that's what he called it anyway. How long until we get there?"

"One day and one half to Gate of Zamdruid," Abadon answered, thinking it wise not to tell Roland the gate itself posed great difficulty in moving forward in their quest for the first artifact. They must pass through the gate to exit the dragon kingdom. Some passed through the gate and some didn't.

Roland looked around. He hadn't been paying attention to the countryside as they went, but noticed now that the pink sun was low on the horizon. This meant the black sun would soon be coming up. They travelled on a pebbled road, the sides flanked by long purple grass. Trees and shrubs dotted the landscape and clumps of wild flowers added color.

As though on que, the pink sun dipped below the horizon at the same time as a black ball rose up into the sky. And just like that, the realm went dark, like someone switched the light off. Utter and complete blackness engulfed them.

"Uhm, Abadon?"

"Hmmm?"

"Uh, how do, uh, I mean, uh, well its pretty dark."

"Yes?"

"Isn't it dangerous to travel like this? I mean, how do the bulls know where they are walking? Aren't they going to trip and fall or something? Shouldn't we wait until daylight to keep going?"

"Bulls can see. Sleep you should. Long night it will be," Abadon instructed Roland.

Really, thought Roland, sleep? He waved his hand in front of his face. At least he thought he waved his hand in front of his face. He couldn't tell. He couldn't see anything. The blackness was absolute. He didn't like it.

"What about the centaurs?" Roland questioned.

"Not worry." Abadon responded.

He continued waving his hand in front of his face, hoping to see even just an outline of something. It was very unnerving and he wished he had some kind of light. Aha! A light! Why didn't he think of that sooner?

"Can you light something so that we can see?"

"No light. Danger. Night creatures it could bring," Abadon said patiently.

A loud snort was heard followed by a growl. "He is afraid of the dark!"

Roland almost jumped out of his skin. Recognizing the voice of King Tartae, Roland wondered when they had rejoined them.

Even in the blackness, Roland knew that his face had turned a deep embarrassed red.

A voice suddenly spoke in his head, soft and fluid, "Ignore the centaur king. He is not himself. He is grieving over the loss of some of his herd. He is only looking to take his anger out on someone. Do not let it be you."

"Who, who said that?" The words tumbled out of Roland's mouth.

"Me," was the response Roland received inside his head.

Well, he thought, didn't that just clear everything up! "Who is me?" he asked aloud. "Abadon, something weird is going on. Someone is talking to me in my head!"

"Yes, but lower your voice you must. Too loud you are."

"What? But..."

The voice came again, quiet and soothing.

"I am Bastian," adding, "You are riding me."

Roland almost asked "who?" again, but stopped when comprehension dawned on him. It was the bull!

"You're the bull? Really? I don't believe it. Someone's jerking my chain. Abadon? Are you doing this?"

"No Roland," Abadon confirmed. "It is your bull. You must keep voice down. Too loud you are."

"Nooooo waaaay!" Roland exclaimed, shifting in the saddle. This was just too bizarre!

"Are you really talking to me in my head," he whispered.

"Yes," the bull whispered back.

"Holy crap on a cracker!" Roland whispered loudly.

"Nooooo, Bastian!" the bull whispered louder.

"No," whispered Roland, "I mean... well uh, never mind."

He didn't know what to say. A huge white bull talking to him telepathically! Way too weird.

Wanting it to keep talking Roland blurted, "What's a Bastian?"

"It is my name."

"Oh, well, it's nice to meet you then Bastian. My name is Roland, Roland White. Uh, thanks for the ride."

"You are most welcome, Roland, Roland White."

"No, just Roland."

"Okay, Just Roland," Bastian replied.

Roland couldn't help it. He snickered. "I meant, just call me nothing but Roland k?"

"My apologies Roland K."

Roland laughed. He decided he could live with Roland K. The grin stayed on his face. If only his friends could see him now, riding a huge white bull that talked to him telepathically! Man, they would go off the deep end.

"It is a great honor to be taking you on this journey Roland K. There were many that wished to be in my place."

"Uh, thanks I guess. Does that mean you volunteered for the job? Do you know where we are going?" Roland wondered if Bastian knew about their quest when it was supposed to be a secret.

"No, I had to win the honor, and I know we only carry you on important realm business."

"What did you have to do?"

"I had to defeat the others. We fought in the ancient way. It is a battle of great proportion. It involves endurance, strength, agility and the spirit of our ancestors. We travel to Tallos Mountain, which is the sacred mountain of my kind. There, we must traverse a maze of caves and caverns that run for many lengths inside. The mountain is full of treacherous and foul creatures. Sometimes you must be fast to escape them, sometimes you must outwit them and sometimes you have to fight them. The first to reach the Horn of Tallos and blow it will reveal the hidden door. There is no other way to get out. Many get lost in the maze and some perish. I found the Horn," Bastian stated proudly.

Roland was completely flabbergasted the bulls would do all that just to give him a ride. He could think of only one thing to say. "I think the honor Bastian, is mine."

Roland had never felt so humbled and a renewed sense of rightness and purpose filled him. He could do no less than give all he had to recover the Timekeeper and return it to Chara before the alignment to save his parents and this realm!

Back in the castle, Eltanin turned away from the wall where he had been watching the three riders and the two centaurs as they left the dragon city. He was happy to see the fire sprite make its way to Roland. He had sent the little creature to the boy thinking it might provide him with some company and a bit of a diversion from the seriousness of the task ahead.

This secret magical chamber allowed him to call forth any part of the kingdom and view it on the wall, much like a movie plays out in a theatre, and he now called forth the road ahead. The way was clear and Eltanin was satisfied their journey through the night would be uneventful.

This room was one of several ways he monitored the realm for which he was guardian. Only one part of the realm was blocked from his view. Rallag. It remained sealed from his sight by Diffandum's dark magic. The evil sorcerer had been destroyed many years ago by Chara's predecessor, Chelios, however, Eltanin suspected the enduring, lingering dark magic was why Rahm chose it for his new lair when he left his castle in Katori.

The ultimate battle between good and evil had begun. Would the realm continue in light and magic, or fall into darkness and chaos? Eltanin sighed. So far, evil seemed to be more than one step ahead.

Slowly leaving the chamber, his heart had never felt so weary or so heavy.

16

Finch

The group carried on in the darkness of the night. Since he wasn't going to be able to sleep yet anyway, Roland passed the time by talking more with Bastian. They talked for hours, and he learned the Cretan bulls were an incredibly old race of beings whose numbers had dwindled after a great battle with a tribe of ogres. The ogres had decided the bulls were a wonderful delicacy and hunted them almost to extinction. After hiding for many centuries, two dragons became aware of their plight and came to their rescue. In return, the bulls vowed to serve the dragons from that day forward.

"Who were the dragons that came to help?"

"Eltanin and Rahm."

"Rahm? The Black Dragon Rahm?" Roland breathed, surprised.

"Yes," Bastian confirmed, "the Black Dragon."

Roland eventually dozed off sometime during the night, and awoke hunched over in the saddle, bright sunshine warming his face. He felt all cramped up and couldn't wait until they stopped so he could stretch his legs.

Yawning and stretching as best he could, he looked around. Startled by squirming against his chest, he pulled open the side of his jacket and the little sprite climbed out. It flew in front of his face, chattering like a chipmunk, its hands waving around as it babbled away, and its tail ribbons flapped and glowed. Roland had completely forgotten about it.

The little guy continued to give Roland a play by play on some story only it could understand. Roland wished he knew what it was saying. It prattled on a bit more before flying right up to Roland's nose, it's pint-sized hands grasped both sides and it proceeded to plant a smacking kiss right on the end, before zipping away.

Eeew, Roland thought rubbing the kiss off. "Did he really have to do that? That was just nasty." He heard Bastian's chuckle in his head.

"It's not funny!" Roland told Bastian, which caused the bull to laugh more, his body shaking, jiggling Roland up and down on his back.

"Stop that," Roland instructed, fighting a smile. "Let's see how funny it is when that little guy does it to you!" Roland threatened, then smiled in satisfaction when the bull instantly stopped laughing. "Aha, not so funny now huh? You know Bastian, if the little guy comes back, I should really give him a name. What do you think?"

Bastian's voice entered his head. "Very good idea. How about Sparky? Or Flame?

Oh, I know, how about Booger?" The bull said before bursting into laughter again.

"A real regular comedian you are," Roland muttered, rolling his eyes. "You are so not helping!"

Thinking for a minute, Roland snapped his fingers. "I know, I think I'll call him Finch!"

"Why Finch?" Bastian wondered.

"Because at home in the summertime, we have these small yellow birds that my mom feeds. They're called Goldfinches. Their color and size kinda remind me of the sprite. What do you think?"

"Finch will work, but I like Booger better!"

At that moment, Abadon turned around and said, "Stop for break soon we will."

Excellent! Roland wondered how the centaurs were doing. They continued to walk ahead of the group in silence. Roland could hear the faint clip clop sound their hooves made on the hard packed earth.

Stopping briefly, they dismounted, had some hasper juice, some snacks and stretched their legs.

All too soon, the break was over. Mounting once more, the trail they were on continued in the distance, winding around trees and shrubs, while a large hill loomed ahead.

For the next hour, Roland told Bastian what it was like growing up in his world. The conversation centred on football, simply because Bastian had a hard time grasping the concept of a game where you tackled each other to catch an oddly shaped ball, simply to get it between two posts.

By the time Roland felt Bastian had a pretty good handle on the game, they were rounding the base of a hill, which dove straight down in a sharp decline. A flat rocky plain covered in gravel, rocks and boulders was ahead. It was a very scarred and broken looking landscape.

As they began the march down into the rocky valley, Bastian told Roland Abadon's bull was called Zantos and was one of the elders, while Sir Balkan's bull was Fand. The bulls were stepping carefully as the small pebbles made the journey difficult, causing their hooves to slip and slide, sending rocks rolling downward, while they struggled to keep their balance. Roland remained quiet so Bastian could concentrate.

They were all relieved when they made it safely down the treacherous incline. Even the centaurs looked tired, catching their breath as they waited for the rest of them. Giant boulders blocked Roland's view, but he had already seen the barren landscape. There was not a speck of grass, a single bush or tree or even one tiny wildflower growing. Come to think of it, he hadn't seen or heard any animals either. It was eerily quiet.

Roland shifted nervously in his seat. Something didn't feel right, like an itch on his back that he couldn't reach to scratch. He shifted again. It felt like something was watching them, as if eyes were drilling holes into the back of his head. Shivering, he looked around. Nothing.

Just then a rumbling noise started. Watching the ground, Roland saw rocks and pebbles vibrating up and down like grasshoppers. Was it an earthquake? Did they have those here?

Just then, Abadon turned in his seat and yelled, "Run!"

"Hang on Roland K!" Bastian shouted in Roland's head and rearing up he pawed the air with his hooves and took off at a gallop.

Roland grabbed onto the sides of the saddle and hung on. Zantos, Fand and their riders disappeared from sight, their camouflage instinct kicking in. Roland hoped Bastian had done the same thing.

The centaurs were far ahead, and were the only thing moving among the rocks until.... The rocks themselves started moving!

At first Roland thought they were just being jolted and jostled but was flabbergasted to see them start joining together like pieces of a jigsaw puzzle. What was going on? What were they doing? Looking from one to another to another, he tried to make sense out of what he was seeing.

It all became disturbingly real as he saw rocky bodies, now with arms and legs, rising up from the dust like zombies coming alive. Stone arms began plucking chunks of rock from the ground. Plunking their findings on top of huge boulder bodies, they were completing their assembly by finding their heads!

Bastian's hooves were flying across the rocky ground, spitting gravel and dust behind him, while Roland bobbed up and down in the saddle like he was sitting on a trampoline. Their speed was impressive and Roland felt a surge of hope. They would make it! They could do it! They could get across this awful terrain and away from the rock giants.

But Roland was so very wrong!

17

Rocky Road

Zantos and Fand skidded to a halt, almost crushing the centaurs against a rock wall formation that burst out of the ground, towering over them, barricading them in. In turn, Bastian and Roland almost crashed into them, Bastian's hooves pedalling backwards in the dust as he desperately tried to stop in time.

But Bastian wasn't able to fully stop and he caught Zantos on the chest, the two of them careening into the wall. Luckily no one was hurt as most of Bastian's forward momentum had slowed down enough that no damage was done. The three bulls snorted and panted, trying to catch their breath, while the centaurs' sides heaved. They were covered in sweat slicked dusty muck.

"Abadon!" Roland cried out in panic. "What is going on?"

Abadon responded, concern filling every nuance of his voice, "Goren. Five hundred years since awake! Very dangerous they are. Much trouble ahead."

For a moment, he looked into the distance and a faraway look came into his eyes as he muttered to himself, "Awoke them someone did."

Roland's heart was pounded in fear. He wanted to snap his fingers in Abadon's face to bring him back to the here and now. What were they supposed to do? They were blocked in.

"We have a fight coming Abadon. They will not be long in assembling themselves and then they will..." Sir Balkan trailed off as they all turned in reaction to the thundering sound of earth shaking steps. Some of the rock giants had finished assembling themselves, like transformer toys, and were bearing down on them with deadly purpose. Large stone feet pounded the ground as they lumbered toward the intruders.

Roland could see that some of them were still forming, not into giants, but disfigured looking animal creatures. To Roland, the twisted images resembled lions and tigers, while more shapes continued to coalesce into grotesque bizarre bears with four arms, moose with sharp pointed rocky fangs, rhinoceros with claws and horns and even walruses with thick hammer shaped flippers and long stone tusks. Some dragged their bodies along the ground because they had no legs. Their facial features were comprised of two eyes and wide gaping mouths. There were no noses or ears. Roars and grunts sounded as they drew closer and closer.

"This is so not good," muttered Sir Balkan as he drew his sword. The high screeching sound of the steel being released from the scabbard was somehow comforting. The centaurs notched arrows into their bows, preparing to fire.

Guttural sounds emanated and echoed from the lipless, toothless mouths of the giants. Was that their language? Were they talking to each other? Were they coordinating their attack? Oh man, they were in very big, very deep trouble.

Sir Balkan slid off Fand's back to take a stance in front of them all as the rock giants came within striking distance. Stepping forward and then to the side, he gave a mighty swing of his sword, taking the knees right out of the first giant, causing it to tumble down to the ground, rocks flying like an exploding volcano. Its face kept appearing and disappearing like it was playing hide and seek with them, as it rolled along the dirt, until it lay unmoving on the ground. Once separated from the body, it became rock once again, useless and inoperable.

As fast as that one broke into pieces, however, more monstrosities appeared. Approaching with heavy lumbering steps, they smashed, stomped and pounded with their feet and fists, trying to squish them like bugs. The centaurs fired their arrows, but they hit the rock bodies and fell uselessly to the ground.

Sir Balkan shouted up at Roland, "Get down and get behind me!"

Roland didn't move. He felt far safer up on Bastian than he would down on the ground, but when Sir Balkan yelled at him again to get down, Roland jumped off Bastian, doing a forward roll when he landed so that he didn't break a leg. Rising up, he coughed, spitting out a mouthful of dirt and dust. He ran over to take cover behind Sir Balkan like he was told.

Abadon sprung off Zantos and the three bulls dropped their camo, but they weren't the same. Roland's eyes almost popped out when he saw the bulls. In place of the calm, gentle creatures they had been riding, were red, snorting, pawing animals, with immense, deadly sharp, curved horns on their heads and spikes on their backs. Their eyes were glowing and they snorted black smoke from their nostrils while massive heads shook back and forth in fury. They were a terrifying sight to behold, furious and ready for battle. Yeah, getting off Bastian was a very good idea!

More rock giants charged and the bulls thundered out to meet them. Their heads swung back and forth, goring the creatures with their horns, while their hooves pawed, stomped and kicked, sending chunks of rock flying way up in the air only to return to the ground like meteors. Those that managed to get by the bulls headed towards them with deadly purpose.

Sir Balkan swung his sword, taking out another one. They were so big that the knees seemed to be the smartest way to take them down. Abadon was on the other side of Sir

Balkan, his staff once more in action and like a Kung Fu master, he was accurate and deadly with it. King Tartae joined the fight, turning his back on any that got close enough and began kicking out with his powerful hind legs. His son joined him, and together they took the knees out of one thrashing close by, sending it splattering to the ground. The rock giant was swinging as it went down, just missing Pentally, who dipped at the last second, dust and debris flying from every desperate swing of its fists.

Rocks and boulders were breaking apart all over the place. Roland had to duck twice so as not to get beaned in the head. He felt so useless. He had no weapon and no idea of how to help.

And then things got really ugly when the animal shaped creatures drew closer. The giants were easier to destroy because they could take out their knees, plus they were very slow and lumbering, but the animals, well they were a different story. They seemed much smarter and much quicker. Roland watched in horror as one resembling a mutated lion began stalking the knight.

Sir Balkan was busy with two giants stomping toward him, one directly in front, the other coming in from the right. He had no way of knowing that a cunning, hump backed lion was making a wide path to the left, crouched low and moving stealthily toward him. Roland knew when it pounced, Sir Balkan would be crushed to death under tons of solid rock.

Looking around desperately, he not only didn't have a weapon, but he had no skill with one even if he did. He yelled and screamed at Sir Balkan to get his attention, but the noise of the smashing, falling rocks was deafening. Roland knew the knight would never hear him.

The lion was getting closer. Its heavy, rocky belly, skimming the ground as it went in low for the kill. A long pebbled tail, swished jerkily from side to side. Ready to pounce, Roland reacted without thinking. With the lion focused solely on its prey, it didn't see Roland running in low, swiping up a chunk of rock as he went and just as the lion pounced, Roland leapt onto the raised foreleg of the lion, propelling himself up onto its back. With all his might, he raised the rock over his head with both hands, bringing it crashing down right between where the head and neck met. The force was enough to sever the lion's head right off. Roland was airborne as the lion lost momentum, tumbling to the ground, its whole body shattering apart upon contact.

Dazed from his own hard landing, Roland rose to his feet, meeting the gaze of Sir Balkan. Time stood still as they stared intently at each other, and then the knight sent Roland a nod, a nod of acknowledgment and a nod of thanks. The knight turned, rejoining the brutal, dusty battle, every swing of his sword connecting with rock.

Sneaking in behind another, one approached, hidden from view. Roland spotted it only because he was at an angle, away from the rest. This creature was like something out of a sci-fi movie, dragging its tail as it moved along the rocky terrain. It seemed to keep gathering pieces of rock to itself as it progressed, getting larger and rounder. It was a lumpy, bumpy, grey mass in the shape of a walrus.

Waving his arms to get its attention, Roland succeeded in changing its direction, moving it away from the rest and toward him. Although it seemed heavy and lumbering, it was upon Roland in no time. Sidestepping to avoid a vicious thrust of the long pointed tusks, it reared its head back for another downward swipe. Reacting instinctively, Roland shrugged out of his coat and threw it up in the air, aiming for the creatures eyes, but he missed and it landed on its forehead. Shaking its head back and forth violently, trying to dislodge the foreign object, it only succeeded in aiding Roland's cause. The shaking sent the bottom of the jacket cascading down its face, covering its eyes and lodging it on a jutting piece of rock.

Blind and confused, not knowing where its target was, Roland did not waste the opportunity and quickly scanned the ground, searching urgently for something to hit it with, when the sound of a great collision reverberated in Roland's ears. Dust filled his eyes, nose and mouth and after hacking up a small dirt pile, Roland wiped his irritated, burning eyes. Bastian stood where the walrus had been, shaking his head to dislodge pieces of rock that clung to his horns. Nothing remained of the walrus but pieces of rock and rubble.

Before Roland could react, the bull spun around and went charging back into the battle. It seemed like it would never end, that the rock creatures would never stop coming, until, finally it did end. When the last rock creature was sent, broken and incapacitated to the ground, silence filled the air. Roland retrieved his jacket from the dust, shaking it out carefully. Taking stock of his surroundings, he saw the bulls, the two centaurs, Sir Balkan and Abadon, coated in dust and breathing heavily from exertion.

Bastian walked over to Roland, his sides heaving and his head hanging low. Thick, brown, gooey sweat dripped off his back and smoke still billowed from his nostrils. Bastian's horns retreated, and the red coat transformed back to white. He looked like himself again, and Roland was relieved to see his friend return to normal.

Roland reached up to rub Bastian's forehead, before moving to the side to stroke his neck, mixing layers of sweat and dirt, producing rusty colored streaks on the bull's white coat.

"Are you alright Bastian?" he asked while looking closely for any signs of blood. He walked to the other side of Bastian, looking carefully for wounds, his hand unwilling to break contact with the soft fur underneath.

"Yes Roland K, I am fine." Bastian answered between pants. "Do you fair well?"

"Yeah, I'm okay," Roland replied, sighing with relief that his new friend was unharmed. "Thank you for saving me Bastian," he said with heartfelt sincerity.

"You are welcome Roland K," the bull answered simply.

Abadon went from one to the other to ensure no one was wounded. Zantos had a nasty gash on his hindquarters, but otherwise they had all been extremely lucky and faired surprisingly well. Roland knew they never would have survived that attack if they hadn't had the bulls.

Abadon picked up his pack from the ground and shaking off the dust, flipped open the top to rummage around. Pulling out a black bottle, he yanked out the cork and walked over to Zantos. He poured a thick, goopy, pale yellow liquid over the bull's wound. Zantos's shanks shook for a moment with pain and then the wound began to heal, the muscle and fur meshing together until all signs of the gash was gone.

Between heavy breaths, King Tartae said, "We must leave this place before they gather again Abadon!"

Abadon nodded in agreement. Turning to the rock wall that blocked their escape, Abadon raised his voice and addressed the wall. "Over is the battle. Let us pass now, you will!"

Standing together, they watched and waited. At the first sign of rumbling, Roland looked around in panic thinking the creatures were forming again, but this time, the rumbling emanated from only one spot. The rocks forming the wall began to shift, some moved one way and some moved the other, creating a large opening for them to pass through.

Warily, eyes darting side to side in case it was a trick or a trap, they each, one by one, passed through. The bulls came last and the wall closed up behind them. In the distance, Roland could see the outline of trees and bushes, meaning an end to this rocky landscape and its deadly inhabitants. He couldn't wait to reach those beacons of nature.

The centaurs didn't hesitate, galloping immediately in the direction of the trees. As tired as everyone was, they were not going to waste any time getting the heck out of there. Using the last of their strength, the bulls too, ran full speed ahead once their passengers boarded.

18

A Fish Out of Water

Roland looked back only once to see the rock wall had vanished. There was no sign of it, nor was there any sign it had even been there. Only harmless looking rocks and boulders dotted the landscape once again. Leaving the rocks behind, Roland was relieved when the bulls stepped onto grass. No one spoke a word and after an hour or so, they stepped out from under a canopy of leafy branches to a new landscape, a new kingdom. Roland's eyes widened when he got a look at the scene spread out before him.

Roland was looking at an ocean, but it wasn't an ocean because there was no water! It was as though the tide sucked all the water away and none of the sea dwellers knew the water was gone! Thousands of small and medium sized multi-colored fish were darting around in the air before scooting in and out of talking sea anemones. There was fish with wings, fish with fur, fish walking on their tails, sweeping the sandy sea floor with small sticks that had little purple octopus attached to the bottom. There was an enormous coral reef rising up to the right of them with flowered sea urchins walking around on long skinny legs carrying baskets full of baby urchins who were squawking and crying.

Following a trail through the sandy bottom, Roland leaned over to see a small field of starfish on stems like flowers, swaying down below as though in a current, while large purple crabs scuttled around using their pincers to cut the stalks of these flowers, carrying their bouquets to a long table made of braided weeds. Hundreds of chairs at the table were quickly filling with scuttling crabs, who, once seated, began pulling apart the starfish flowers, sharing and eating hungrily. Large and small seashells in various shapes and colors walked around the sandy bottom, bumping into each other. Rumbling and grumbling could be heard. Watching closely, Roland saw two little old men with wrinkled, sagging, drooping scrunched up faces pop out of the shells after a slow motion crash, argue loudly with each other. Roland was so spellbound, he almost fell off.

"Where are we?" he asked Bastian quietly. Their pace had slowed and Roland could hear Abadon talking to a boat sized whale that was swimming in the air along beside him.

"We are in the Kingdom of Nautilus. It is our waterless ocean. It is not very wide so we will cross soon, but it is hundreds of miles long."

"Wow, this is really amazing," Roland said gawking at everything around him. "Are there, like, killer sharks here too?"

"I don't know what a shark is Roland K, but there are many dangerous and deadly fish here. They tend to stay to the shadows during the day, so it is safe for us to cross now, however, never cross Nautilus during the night. No one ever crosses during the night." The enormous bull gave a shudder.

Bastian was right, and it didn't take long to get across. Climbing a steep bank, they continued on, following a worn path through brush and shrubs, until they finally reached a narrow stream. Here they stopped to have a much needed break.

Abadon announced they would not only stop here, but rest for a while as well. As soon as their riders got off, the saddles disappeared and the bulls trotted to the stream, filling up on the fresh, clean cold water with loud slurps before splashing in to wash off all the dirt and dust.

The centaurs moved farther up the stream before they took a much needed drink as well, then copied the bulls, wading in to wash off.

Abadon, Roland and Sir Balkan sat on a round mossy bank, quenching their own thirst from water skins.

Abadon looked over at Roland and raised an eyebrow.

"What?" Roland asked blinking.

"Bombard me with questions you are not?"

Roland shrugged his shoulders, "Nah, I guess I figured you would fill me in when you were ready. You are going to fill me in aren't you?"

"Ha," said Abadon in triumph, "Knew I did you would ask a question!"

"That's not fair," protested Roland, and then smiled when he realized Abadon was only teasing.

Sir Balkan stood up. "I need to go wash off as well." Meeting Roland's look, he leaned over to give him an awkward pat on the back. "You did real good back there kid."

Before Roland could respond, he had turned to walk toward the stream.

"Read scroll now we will," Abadon said after another big swallow of water.

"Yeah, okay. How do I know which one it is?" Roland asked as he rummaged around in the knapsack lying at his side. Something made him think of Damone's tear and his heart started beating like a caged bird. What if it fell out of his coat pocket when he threw his jacket on that walrus and was laying back on that rocky ground? Patting his pockets quickly, he sighed in relief. It was still there. Good thing the little sprite hadn't been in there during the battle because he probably would have been seriously injured. Roland wondered where the little guy was.

Glancing around, he saw the bulls laying on the grass while the centaurs stood together at the edge of the flowing water, talking to each other quietly.

Unhooking the bag, Abadon told him they would read the scrolls in the order of the suns, so Roland reached inside and pulled out a scroll with a yellow ribbon tied around it. Handing the scroll to Abadon, he leaned back on his hands, waiting as Abadon untied the ribbon and slowly unrolled it.

Roland could see fancy scripted words flowing across the page.

"Destroy this we must," Abadon shook the paper lightly in the air, "when finished. Remember words Roland. Very important this is."

Roland nodded his understanding.

Holding it out, Abadon read it to Roland quietly. When he was finished, he absently handed the scroll to Roland before standing up and walking away, deep in thought. Roland took the scroll and read it over and over again, memorizing each and every word.

Looking away, he replayed the words in his head just to make sure he had it right and had it memorized.

The words made absolutely no sense to him and his heart sank. He whispered the words to himself.

An artifact both rare and true
Taken from the soul of two.

One who is worthy can use its might
A sacrifice given of heart and light.

The sands of time flow through the glass
Blood of the innocent magic shall pass.

Search for a cave deep underground
Beware Sulandow who prowls around.

Blades of steel only cause strife
Pierce of sound can save your life.

The words etched themselves into Roland's brain. He nodded his head to Abadon upon his return, indicating he was done with it. Handing it to Abadon, the warlock swiped his right hand over the paper as thought wiping dirt off it, whispering something as he did so. Roland expected it to burst into flames but it didn't. There was no time. It just disintegrated. Poof! There was nothing left in Abadon's hands but tiny ashes. No flames, no fire, no small explosion, nothing. Just one minute it was paper, the next a small pile of ash. Holding his hand up, the breeze caught the ashes, playfully throwing them into the air.

Turning, Abadon gave a sharp piercing whistle and the rest of the group rose slowly to join them.

"Eat now. Travel Zamdruid Gate we will."

The centaurs pulled packs off their backs, rummaged around, pulling out queer looking fruits and nuts, which they quickly began eating.

Sitting with Abadon and Sir Balkan, Roland didn't recognize a single thing he was eating. The best he could do was make guesses. Sir Balkan pulled apart and passed around small chunks of black bread. It didn't look appetizing, but tasted really good, having a very nutty flavor to it.

Next, there was weird looking smooth, baseball sized, green things that Abadon passed over to Roland and Sir Balkan, keeping one for himself. Watching how Abadon ate his, Roland followed suit and bit into it, peel and all. The outside and the inside of it didn't change in texture. It was all kind of thick and rubbery but wow! It tasted just like bacon. It was awesome! Roland found out it was called syca. Bacon anything was delish, so he hoped his bag contained a whole bunch. He figured he could probably eat ten of them.

Lastly, there was six inch long skinny white things called olas, that when peeled, tasted like mandarin oranges and marble sized black beads called maxels that tasted like pumpkin pie. He loved pumpkin pie and popped them into his mouth like popcorn.

All in all, it was really good and Roland was stuffed when he was done. Nothing had to be cooked, so eating didn't take long.

"Assuming we pass Zamdruid Gate, what is our destination after that?" Sir Balkan asked.

"Through the Gate we must first get. Worry about destination after."

Roland saw King Tartae frown at those words, but before the centaur could comment, Abadon got them back on the road.

Roland replayed the scroll in his head numerous times just to make sure it was stuck in there good. His thoughts turned to Sir Balkan's comment about Zamdruid Gate. What did he mean by the word "assuming"?

He decided to ask Abadon, and was told the Gate only let those it deemed worthy pass through. When Roland questioned further, he was informed that should they fail to pass, the consequences wouldn't be good and their quest would be over. He would say no more after that.

The rest of the day passed uneventfully. Roland dozed off and on in the saddle as Bastian trudged along. The little fire sprite returned, waking Roland from a restless sleep, to buzz and chatter in his face.

"Well hello little guy, where have you been?" Roland yawned and rubbed his blurry eyes.

Frantic chattering followed Roland's question.

"Really? Wow, that's fascinating!" Roland replied with a smile. The sprite was such a bizarre little dude.

"Do you understand what it is saying to you?" Bastian asked in surprise.

"Not a word." Roland replied.

Bastian laughed.

The sprite landed on Roland's shoulder and began stroking his neck. With no fingernails, just those rounded bulbous tips on the ends of his fingers, it tickled. Roland lifted his hand and shooed him off.

Hovering in front of Roland's face, it pointed at Roland's chest.

"Did you want to go back into my pocket?"

Chattering, it nodded its head vigorously.

Obviously the little guy could understand Roland, so he decided to ask, "Do you have a name?"

More obscure, nonsensical chatter followed. "You know I can't understand you right?"

The nod returned.

"But you can understand me can't you?"

Another nod.

"Well, would you mind if I gave you a name?"

A third nod.

"I was thinking Finch might be a good one. What do you think?"

The sprite hovered quietly in the air for a moment before pointing at itself with its finger and gave a great big grin. In an excited high pitched, squeaky voice, it tapped its chest with one hand and said slowly, "Ffiinnch?"

"Yes, yes," Roland grinned. "You Finch, me Roland." Roland said, putting his hand on his own chest.

Tapping the top of its head this time with the flat of its hand, it said with a big smile while confirming its name, "Finch!"

"That's right!" Roland grinned ear to ear. What a smart little guy.

Flying right in Roland's face, it tapped Roland on the nose and said very slowly, "Wwwwolann?"

Bastian giggled. Roland ignored him.

"No, Rrrrroland," he corrected Finch, dragging out the r sound.

"Wwwwolann," the fire sprite imitated, dragging out the w.

Shrugging his shoulders, Roland said, "close enough little guy."

Clapping his hands, Finch spun excitedly in the air, the red ribbons billowed out, catching Roland under the chin, giving him the feeling he had just walked into a spider web.

Finch pointed at Roland's chest again, then stretched his little mouth out in a great big yawn. Getting the point, Roland opened the side of his jacket, and Finch swept in, pulling open the inside pocket, which he obviously now claimed as his, and quickly crawled inside. He shifted around, pushing at the sides, then made three circles before plopping down, curling up and falling asleep. Roland shook his head wishing he could fall asleep that easily.

Roland turned his attention back to Bastian, "I have to tell yah dude, I sure am glad that you're along on this quest. I don't know what we would have done against those Goren rock things without you guys!"

"I am honored to be a part of this, Roland K, for as long I can."

"What do you mean by that?" Roland asked anxiously.

"Master Abadon told Zantos our journey will end long before yours will. Do not worry Roland K. I will be with you for as long as I am allowed. May I ask what a dude is?"

Roland knew Bastian was trying to sidetrack him, and since he didn't want to think about continuing on this quest without Bastian, he decided to play along. He explained it was just a figure of speech. Bastian thought it was funny and wanted to know more figures of speech, so Roland explained current meanings of words like "sick, bazinga, cool, sweet, jam, balm and dawg". Bastian found this all to be very funny and extremely strange.

"But if a word already is a word, why do you give it another word instead? I really don't understand Roland K. It is very confusing."

"Ah, don't worry about it Bastian. That's just the way it is."

"Okay. Would it be hot then for me to say, you are the bazinga Roland K?"

Roland burst out laughing. "Not quite Bastian. First, it's *cool*, not *hot*, and you could say, you the balm, or you the dawg," Roland clarified.

Under all the joking, Roland's heart felt heavy at the fact he and Bastian might have to part at some point on this journey. He had assumed he would have Bastian with him all the way. This big, strong bull had given him a real sense of confidence. He now felt scared, small, weak and sad.

Bastian's voice filled his head again.

"I know what you are thinking Roland K. I can feel your body tensing. You must realize that whether I am with you or not, you will not be doing this alone. You have help. Rely on those who are with you and trust in yourself. Follow your instincts and remember that you are here on this quest for a reason. Look at what you did against the Goren. You didn't hesitate to fight. I know you surprised Sir Balkan, which is an even greater feat than defeating those rock creatures!" Roland gave a small smile at this and Bastian continued, "I do not know what this quest is about, but I know it is very important, and I also know Eltanin is a very wise and powerful Guardian. If he believes in you, then so do I. You have become my friend, Roland K. I know you will accomplish whatever it is you have to do!"

"I hope you are right Bastian," Roland muttered, wishing he had the same belief and confidence in himself. He wished he could tell Bastian everything. He wanted to tell him about his parents, the Prophecy, the scrolls, the Spirit Dragons, everything. He knew Bastian would understand it all, and know just what to say to make him feel better, but he knew he wasn't allowed and so he kept quiet, falling into his own thoughts as they trudged along.

The yellow sun fell, leaving the sky to the blue one. It cast a warm, soothing early afternoon glow over the realm. Off in the distance he could see a long, black shadow extending across the horizon, from one side to the other. Another shadow grew out of the first, towering straight into the sky, so high it was obscured by the clouds. Whatever it was, it was ginormous!

"Is that Zamdruid Gate I can see in the distance?" he wondered aloud.

"Yes Roland K, it is."

"Have you been there before?"

"I have not. I have had no need to leave the dragon kingdom of Dragayo."

"Do you know anything about this gate?"

"Only that many avoid the gate and go the long way around."

"Why?"

"Because some have gone to the gate and never returned."

"Well that's just great," Roland said grouchily. "Why didn't we just go around it then too?"

"I think it is because it would take too many weeks to travel around the wall that spreads out from the gate. You can see the wall from here. It is many, many miles long, longer even than the Kingdom of Nautilus."

Roland scratched his head. "I wonder what we have to do in order to pass through. Do you think maybe we have to solve, like a riddle or something?"

"I do not know Roland K."

"I guess we will find out soon enough." Roland said as the shadow loomed ahead. Butterflies tickled his stomach as they drew closer with every step.

19

Eye See You

From the distance, Roland could see they were travelling to a colossal tree. Branches grew out the sides, so thick and so numerous, they had entwined themselves into an impenetrable hedged wall fifty feet high. The wall went out in both directions, with the massive tree standing like a sentinel in the middle.

Reaching the tree, the trunk itself was as wide as a house. Mammoth sized branches hung down low and the wind stirred them enough to give brief glimpses of two large wooden doors hidden underneath, doors that seemed to have been built out of the trunk itself. Roland moved his head up and down and then side to side, trying to get a better view, but it was hard to tell for sure because he could only get small, brief glimpses through the draping branches that swept the ground.

Looking up, way up, Roland could see no end to the height of the tree. It was completely lost in the clouds.

Halting in front and dismounting, the group stood silently. No one moved and no one spoke. Roland shuttered at what he saw and Bastian gave his great head a nervous shake.

Each and every single leaf, on each and every branch, had an eye on it.

Branches bobbed up and down gently. As quiet and deadly as a swooping, striking eagle, branches unexpectedly swung down low, encasing each one of them in a separate green cage. Roland's heart fluttered in panic as the eyes scanned him from top to bottom, like a hospital scanner, inspecting him carefully, before lifting its canopy of leafy eyes up and away. Zantos gave a snort when his branch got to close and touched his flank.

When all the branches had retreated, Roland whispered to Abadon, "What happens now?" He was afraid to speak any louder just in case there were ears hidden somewhere too.

Without answering, Abadon only parted the hanging curtain of branches in front of him and stepped inside, dropping them behind, disappearing from view.

Roland transferred his weight from one foot to the other. Looking around at the others to see if they should follow or just stay put, he got his answer when first the centaurs followed, then Sir Balkan. Roland felt a nudge on his back from Bastian. Taking a few steps toward the hanging branches, he stopped and turned.

"Are you coming too?"

"Yes Roland K, I shall be right behind you." Bastian confirmed, and feeling relieved, Roland parted the branches very carefully, not wanting to touch any of the disturbing, unsettling eyeballs, ducking underneath.

Once inside, the hanging branches created a dimly lit, sheltered hut.

Abadon was standing directly in front of elaborately detailed doors. Each door was immense, big enough for even the largest of the realms' beings to pass through, and was decorated in an incredible array of mythical creatures. The detail and obvious talent in whoever created it was evident to even Roland who had never carved as much as a pointed stick. Stepping forward, Roland reached out a hand, tracing his finger along a miniature engraved version of Bastian, before moving on to another that was identical to Eltanin. Every creature, being and person of the realm seemed to be represented on this door. He saw knights in armour, fairies, elves, goblins griffins, unicorns and many others he didn't recognize. He even saw a person sculpted to look exactly like Abadon.

"Whoa, this is amazing!" Roland whispered reverently. "Who made this?"

Abadon turned to him with a raised eyebrow. "Tree made, of course."

"Oh yes, of course," Roland smacked himself in the forehead. "What a dumb question. I should have known that, because our trees at home paint murals on buildings and carve museum pieces all the time."

The sarcasm wasn't lost on Abadon, who only frowned for a moment before deciding to ignore Roland's comment. "Address the Gate you must Roland. Introduce yourself. Ancient the tree is. Respectful you must be. Passage through you request."

Roland jolted when two giant eyes simultaneously popped open, one on each door. Filled with swirling, moving rainbows of color, like a great wind was blowing inside, blanket sized eyelids blinked slowly, the gaze considered each one of them in turn, observing for uncomfortably long moments, before dropping heavy lids as though bored and going to sleep. Roland decided it was okay if it went to sleep. Those huge eyes were way too spooky and weird and gave him giant goosebumps.

A voice suddenly spoke from above, echoing around the leafy branches, sounding like the splitting and cracking of old wood.

"Who disturbs the Gate?"

For a moment, no one moved, not even to breathe.

Roland yanked on Abadon's arm. "Why couldn't we just go around this thing?" He whispered.

"Too many days lost to go around. Now," Abadon gave Roland a nudge with his elbow, "do as I said."

But Roland wasn't doing anything of the sort. "Why do I have to? Can't you? What if I say something wrong, or he doesn't like me or, well, I don't know, but can't someone else talk to it?" his voice rising frantically.

Just then Finch crawled out of Roland's coat pocket, appearing under Roland's jaw, chattering like crazy, waving his arms while he climbed around to stand on Roland's shoulder. "Sshhh Finch, be quiet!" Roland murmured to the fire sprite, but it continued its tirade, getting louder and louder. "You're gonna get us in trouble Finch! Sshhh." Roland put his finger to his lips, trying to shush the sprite.

But Finch only got more agitated, fluttering around Roland's face, poking at his nose and cheeks, his chatter very high pitched in his anxiousness.

"What is it Finch? What's the matter? Slow down." Roland hissed, trying to wave Finch out of his face. Maybe if he could figure its problem, it would be quiet, but it just wouldn't stop.

"Finch, if you don't settle down, I'm gonna have to, well, I don't know, do something, now behave!" Roland muttered sternly, but the fire sprite ranted uncontrollably, before abruptly freezing in mid chatter. Making eye contact with Roland, Finch hovered in the air directly in front of Roland's face, his little wings making a slight whirring sound. All chattering and gestures stopped, and he stared at Roland with his buggy eyes the size of saucers. Just when Roland was going to ask again what was wrong, Finch, not taking his eyes off Roland, slowly and deliberately pointed upward with one tiny finger.

Roland raised an eyebrow in question, before his eyes followed Finch's finger upward. He was just in time to see a large, bare branch looking exactly like a brown, dried up, skeleton hand, lunge down and snag him up in its clutches, whipping him off his feet and rushing up into the branches above with its prize.

Feeling like he had just been scooped up like dog poo, Roland struggled desperately, twisting and turning and pulling at the bony fingers, trying to pry them open. But the grip was firm and snug. He was going up higher and higher and higher. Finch zig zagged along, ducking and bobbing to escape the same branches tearing at Roland as they whizzed by. Rising at an incredible speed,

Roland covered his face with his arms to protect it from being shredded like cheese.

I am going to be tree food, he thought to himself. That's what was happening. The tree was going to dump him into a great big mouth at the top and he would digest in its bark for a thousand years. A zillion eyes would watch as tiny flecks of skin were peeled off and eaten one piece at a time.

This horrible thought gave him a renewed sense of urgency to escape, and he yanked, pulled, pried and tugged at the rough, long, knot covered fingers, but it was no use. He couldn't budge them an inch.

Looking down, he could barely see the top of the wall, his friends nonexistent below, hidden under the draping branches. The wall was now nothing but a teeny, tiny shadow. He realized escaping might not be such a good idea after all. He quickly changed from struggling frantically to hanging on anxiously. He had no desire to fall now. He would be like a bug on a windshield if he fell now. Splat! The end! Finished! Caput! Done like dinner! Toasted! Expired! Terminated!

The hand's ascent began to slow and then stopped completely, gently swaying up and down. Finch quickly landed on Roland's shoulder, strangely silent. Roland was so high up he was finding it hard to breathe, like someone was sitting on top of his chest. Glancing down, he could see nothing below but white swirling clouds. Holy crap, he thought, feeling dizzy. Looking up, he was still surrounded by thick branches, allowing only peeks of light through. He had no idea how high he was, but what he did know was that he was not even at the top of this thing yet.

Looking at the enormous trunk directly in front of him, he thought he detected some movement. Yes, there it was again! The bark was moving, contorting and stretching weirdly. Roland would have scrambled backward if he could, but since he had no wriggle room, he could only watch, shrinking himself into the back of the bony hand as much as possible.

But Roland didn't stay that way for long and didn't even notice that he was leaning forward to watch in amazement as an old, wrinkled, wizened wooden face stretched and shifted until it was protruding out of the tree trunk. But there was something wrong with it. Roland could see the nose and wide, thick lips with wrinkled cheeks and deep indents where the eyes would be, but that was where the problem was. There were no eyes!

Giant leaves layered around the face like long, green flowing hair with a matching beard, eyebrows and a mustache. These were the only leaves that didn't have any eyes on them. Crackling and splintering sounds came out of the large mouth as it began to move. Deep, echoing words forming on the lips.

"Who is at my door!" it bellowed, blowing Roland back into the twisted, gnarled fingers. Finch quickly flew to Roland, grabbing the collar of his jacket to tug him forward, trying to hang onto him so he didn't blow away.

Realizing this wasn't helping, Finch returned to Roland's shoulder, spreading his little arms out on Roland's neck in an awkward hug, and tucked his face in behind Roland's earlobe.

Thinking quickly, knowing he was in big trouble, Roland replied, "Oh Great One, my sincere apologies for not answering sooner. You see, I was so awe struck by the wondrousness of the sight of your great gate, I was unable to form words for a moment. My name is Roland White. I am here to ask if my friends and I could please pass through." Crossing his fingers, he waited, hoping those weren't the last words he ever uttered.

Finch left Roland's shoulder to land on his arm tugging at his sleeve. Looking down, Roland saw a candle size flame in the palm of the little sprite's hand. Now what was he doing?

Roland's eyes widened when he realized what Finch was suggesting. Shaking his head no, Roland leaned over and blew it out. The flame immediately returned, and the sprite chattered anxiously. "No Finch!" Roland said, blowing it out again.

"What is going on?" the tree bellowed again as a branch from above plunged down and thousands of eyes looked at Roland and Finch. They both froze.

Realizing he needed to answer, Roland surprised himself when the words tumbled out of his mouth before he could stop them. "This little guy here, uh, his name is Finch. You see sir, he's a, uhm, fire sprite and I think he wants to start you on fire. But he doesn't know what he's doing sir," Roland said quickly, "you see, he's trying to save me!" Roland snapped his mouth shut before any more foolish words could come out of it.

Finch smacked himself in the forehead with his tiny little hand. Roland wanted to do the same thing to himself. What was wrong with him! Why didn't he just keep his mouth shut? Roland squirmed in the branch's grasp. Finch smacked himself in the head again.

"Okay, okay, I get it. Stop being a drama queen Finch. I'm sorry," Roland said out of the side of his mouth. There was nothing Roland could do about it now but wait and see what happened.

Well, what happened was something Roland never would have guessed in a million years. The tree began shaking violently. Deep rumbling sounds mixed with the swishing of moving leaves. Finch immediately dive bombed back into Roland's pocket. What was going on? Oh boy, he really did it now. He made it very, very angry! What was it going to do to him?

Roland waited in terror, clutching at the hand holding him, his knuckles white and his eyes wide with fear. The rumbling and shaking continued but nothing was happening to him. He hadn't been flung to the ground or squeezed to death or eaten. He was completely mystified, until the light went on when he saw sap dripping from the eyeless sockets and down its cheeks like tears. Tears! It was tears! The tree was laughing so hard it was crying!

Roland was so relieved, he wanted to laugh too. The stress and tension of the last few moments trickled out in a slight chuckle, then a small giggle, and then Roland was laughing too. He laughed so hard he snorted, which only made him laugh harder. The tree and the boy laughed and laughed and laughed.

When the laughter finally subsided, Roland wiped at his own tears, while the tree took a minute to catch its breath. Roland held his own, waiting to see what the tree would do next. He had no choice after all. Where could he go? He was miles up in the air amongst branches and leaves with millions of eyes staring unblinking at him, conversing with a giant tree, while being held in front of its face like an ice cream cone. The whole situation was so bizarre, he felt like laughing again, but held it in and waited.

The eyeless face finally regained its composure, stroking branches along its face to wipe away the sappy tears. The eyebrows frowned and a thin side branch swept in to stroke the tree's bushy, leafy beard while he spoke.

"It has been many years since I have laughed and never have I ever laughed like that before. I thank you for that Roland White. It has been many more years since I have had a small boy at my gate. Flattery will not gain you passage through my gate little one, so don't give me anymore of it. Now, tell me why I should not simply crush you and all your small friends below and return to my business?"

Roland knew he had one shot and one shot only to make this good. Thinking frantically, his mouth opened and closed a few times like a hungry koi fish in a pond. He could think of nothing to say, finally deciding on simply telling the truth!

"My name is Roland White. I came to the Realm of Abraxas from earth. Some believe that I can save the realm from the Black Dragon, Rahm."

"Really," the tree replied. "And who, pray tell, thinks you can do this?"

"Well, Eltanin," Roland answered, before adding quickly, "and the Spirit Dragons."

Fascinated, the tree rumbled. "Very interesting. Tell me more!"

And so there Roland sat, in a twisted, knotted tree hand, a zillion miles up in the sky talking to a giant tree. He told his story from beginning to end. He left out only one thing, the scrolls.

When Roland finally finished, the tree asked, "How is it you would do all this for this realm? Why would you sacrifice your life for creatures and beings you do not know? Answer this!" the tree demanded.

Roland thought for a moment scratching his head. "I guess because I would never forgive myself if I walked away knowing the realm would be destroyed if I did. It's about doing the right thing no matter the cost, and helping this realm and these creatures, well, it's the right thing to do," he finished with a shrug.

The tree pondered this for a moment. "A very brave little soul you are young one. I sense dragon magic in you. Why is that?"

Roland explained to the tree about his ancestor, what he did, and how he received the Spirit of the Dragon. And then he talked about being afraid, how he was worried that he would let everyone down, and how it would be his fault if death and destruction ensued. He talked about his parents and how worried he was about them and how sad he felt.

The tree was quiet. And then he told Roland a story of his own. The story of how he came to be "the Gate". He said that once he had been a young sapling, having a great time exploring the realm when he came upon a battle between a young witch and an old warlock. The witch was losing and in desperation, asked for his help in defeating the warlock. He told her he did not worry himself about the affairs of other beings nor care about their problems. He then kept going.

Much time had passed when the young witch found him, in fact, it turned out she had hunted him down. She told him that because he did not help, the warlock had destroyed many innocent creatures in his quest for power, and had the sapling assisted her, those lives could have been saved. She had defeated the evil warlock, but at a great cost to others. She punished the tree by planting his leg roots right where he stood and told him he would never explore again.

He would forever remain here in this spot, his roots would never again play in the earth of the kingdoms. And because he had not wanted to be involved, he now had no choice but to be to be involved, for his job at the Gate never allowed rest from travellers seeking passage through his trunk.

His trunk and roots had never taken another step from that day on and his heart yearned to resume his travels. More than anything, he wished to once again walk upon the grass, to stop and water his roots at a crystal clear stream, to climb a mountain or to feel an ocean storm blow through his branches and upon his face. It would be the most wonderful thing in the world. Instead, he became the gatekeeper. It was his duty to decide who was worthy and who was not worthy to pass through. He told Roland not a day went by over these many millennium that he didn't wish he had stopped and helped.

"In a way, Roland White, we had the same decision to make. I chose to walk away. But you, young one, are choosing to stay and help. It has been most interesting meeting you. I thank you for providing a noteworthy break from a normally boring day." The hand holding him began lowering him away from the now sad looking face. The voice of the tree spoke one last time, drifting down to Roland, "If you ever need my assistance, little one, call my name, and I will come."

"But what is your name?" Roland shouted back up. He received no reply. "Sir? Sir? What is your name?" Roland yelled as loud as he could. Nothing. He was already too far away.

When he was almost at the bottom, he saw relief bloom across the faces of the group and Bastian instantly entered Roland's head to ask if he was okay. The branch set him down gently and Roland watched the branch return to its place among the thousands of others, before assuring Bastian he was okay.

Wordlessly, Abadon took out some salve from his bag and dealt with the many shallow cuts Roland had received on his face and hands from his trip up the tree. He felt the cuts healing together and after a few sips of water, he felt almost normal again.

The group had waited patiently, but now huddled around Roland, asking questions so fast and furious, Roland didn't know which to answer first. He didn't get a chance to answer any however, because just then a deep, loud groan of wood sounded. Turning as one, they all watched as the massive doors shifted forward before slowly sliding open.

The group all turned to stare at Roland, their mouths hanging open in surprise. Giving a great big grin, he said gleefully, "You all better be careful or you will have gross, slimy swally's crawling in those open traps!" Four mouths snapped shut and Roland grinned even wider.

As they gathered up the supplies that had been unloaded on the ground, he was surprised to learn from Abadon he had been gone for over three hours. As they headed to the open gate, Abadon put his hand briefly on Roland's shoulder. When Roland looked up, Abadon said proudly, "Very well you did!"

Roland gave a nod of acknowledgment. Inside, his confidence bloomed. Maybe, just maybe, he thought to himself, he could do this after all.

Bastian and Roland started through the open gate and Roland smiled at the thousands of eyes that winked at him as he passed by.

It took them almost an hour to traverse the twisted, winding path through the wide trunk of the old tree. Inside it smelled of cedar, making Roland feel safe and secure, reminding him of home and his own bedroom. He wasn't sure why, because he knew his room smelled mostly of stinky socks, but for whatever reason, it did and it was comforting.

Birds flew from branch to branch, twittering and tweeting but remained elusive, never allowing themselves to be seen. The darkness inside the tree was kept at bay by thousands of fist sized fireflies. Roland got a quick look at one when it landed on the top of Bastian's head. It was round with black and white stripes and tiny wings that made Roland wonder how those wings were strong enough to allow it to fly. It had bulbous eyes and a really long skinny nose that swayed back and forth as though it was searching for food.

Bastian gave his head a shake. "That tickles," he told Roland. Roland laughed and kept trying to get another close look at one, but they hovered too far overhead. It was like walking in the dark with a thousand candles shining down from above. Roland felt like he was wrapped in a nice warm blanket on a cold night in front of a roaring fire. He would have been very happy to stay in here, it felt safe.

When they reached the end, another set of enormous doors silently slid open and they passed through the trunk and out the other side. The green sun had gone, replaced by a soft pink light, signalling the day was almost done. This side of the tree was like being in a huge solarium, filled with a forest of trees and packed full of plants, flowers and shrubs, all blooming with a variety of colors, shapes and sizes.

The group travelled quietly, the only sounds were those of chirping birds and buzzing insects.

They followed an obscure grassy path through the trees and bush for another hour before Abadon called a halt and a fifteen minute rest. King Tartae grumbled and mumbled something about just sitting around for three hours. Abadon gave him a stern look and reminded him Roland hadn't had the same rest they did. King Tartae turned away in a huff. Roland looked at Pentally, but the young prince turned away as well. Roland thought he looked embarrassed at his father's behaviour. Roland didn't blame him. His father, so far, was not a likeable guy… well horse…. Well combination horse/guy.

Dismounting, Abadon handed Roland a chicken flavored syca which he ate hungrily and then two tubes of the white olas. Today they didn't taste like oranges, but one tasted of sweet, juicy green grapes and the other kind of like a coconut.

Sir Balkan approached.

"Abadon, don't you think it's time we know where we are going?" He asked, pulling his sword from its sheath to examine the blade, turning it this way and that, rubbing here and there at invisible dirt.

"Right Sir Balkan is. Centaurs, join us now you should." Abadon knelt down on the grassy knoll. Roland sat down cross legged and placed his elbows on his knees, resting his chin on entwined fingers. Sir Balkan stood, as did King Tartae. Prince Pentally, after a moment's hesitation, sank down on his four legs beside Roland, not meeting his father's angry stare. Roland looked over at him, surprised, but the prince did not meet his gaze.

"From here," Abadon stated, "we travel to the Sand Kingdom."

Pentally was so surprised that not only did his mouth fall open, but he started to rise before literally plunking back down onto his haunches, his butt hitting the forest floor with a thud. The centaur prince visibly swallowed and Roland recognized fear on his face.

Well that can't be good!

Roland found his appetite flee. He put the remaining syca into his jacket pocket for Finch, who squealed in delight. Searching the rest of the faces, he saw Sir Balkan frowning, Tartae scowling and the three bulls shifted their bulky weight from one hoof to another. Since they all seemed very uncomfortable with Abadon's announcement, Roland realized their quest to recover the first of six artifacts was not going to be as easy as passing through the Zamdruid Gate.

Sir Balkan was the first to speak. "Why do we travel there Abadon? I thought we were making our way to the black dragon."

"Yes," Abadon assured the knight, "important stop this is. Sand Kingdom we must go. Lead us you will. Been there you have."

"You didn't answer my question Abadon!" Sir Balkan stated, pulling his shoulders back and crossing his arms, a scowl on his face.

Abadon rose gracefully from his knees, pulling his shoulders back as well, causing him to tower over Sir Balkan. Looking down he said in no uncertain terms, "Defeat Rahm imperative to save all. Reason why Sand Kingdom? Part of plan and not necessary to know right now. Trust me you must. If not, fail we will! Know everything in time. Patience."

Abadon's anger was palpable and a heavy silence fell over them.

"Very well Abadon, we will do it your way," sighed Sir Balkan then added, "for now." Motioning to Fand, he climbed onto his bull and started down the trail, disappearing when he rounded a bend through the trees.

The rest followed slowly.

20

The Sand City

They continued on, stopping twice for quick breaks. They left the small forest behind, travelled through a grassy meadow and up and over small rolling hills. Roland knew they had reached their destination when the grass abruptly stopped like an invisible line drawn on the ground. One minute it was green, the next there was nothing to see but sand, sand and more sand. Dunes broke the flat landscape like brown waves stranded on the shore. More waves flowed over and then they too were stranded. Layers upon layers formed in a frozen replica of a windy sea. It was hollow and desolate looking, but somehow compelling and beautiful at the same time.

They stopped at the edge, staring out at the vastness of the red desert.

"Sand Kingdom this is," said Abadon with a wide sweep of his hand. "Sir Balkan know. Been here before he has. Tell us he will."

"Well, not many have been here and lived to tell about it. This desert is home to beings known as sand waifs. During the day, they rise up from below the desert and hunt using sand traps. They stay underground at night because that is when they are the most vulnerable and can be killed. Tell me where you want to go and I will guide us from here."

"To City of Amrah we go."

"Are you sure Abadon?" Sir Balkan asked quietly.

"Retrieve something we must. Very important to quest it is."

"I have been to the City of Amrah. This is a very dangerous city. The sand waifs are vile and disgusting creatures."

When he received no response, he sighed. "Alright then. Everyone," he said loudly to ensure he had their attention, "wrap something over your noses and mouths, otherwise sand will fill your lungs and you will suffocate," he ordered.

Roland gulped. *Why does it just keep getting better and better?*

Roland was bumped out of his musings by Bastian's head. "This is where we must part my friend. My role in your journey is over for now. I would like to continue, but Zantos says this is where we must part."

Roland was devastated. Quickly turning to Abadon, he questioned, "Are the bulls not coming with us?"

Giving his head a shake, Abadon answered, "On foot we must travel."

"But, why? Why can't they come?"

"Too large they are. Dangerous it is for them to come." Walking over to Zantos, Abadon stroked the bull's white neck. "Old friend, safely home you travel. Thank you, I do."

Zantos nodded his massive head. Unloading his packs, Abadon gave his bull one last look and a nod before Zantos turned and walked away.

Sir Balkan said his own good-byes quietly while he unloaded Fand, who then followed Zantos.

Roland rested his forehead against the lowered head of Bastian. Rubbing the side of Bastian's face, Roland didn't know what to say or how to express how sad he was that his friend was leaving him.

As they stood like that, Sir Balkan unloaded the packs from Bastian and then left them alone. Roland was thankful for that.

"I shall miss you my friend." Roland whispered.

"We might meet again on this quest of yours' Roland K." Roland gave a small smile at the name. "If not, I shall be waiting for you back at the stables. Return soon so that we might ride together again. Be safe. I have been honored."

With that, Bastian stepped back, turned and followed the other two. Roland stood and watched Bastian depart. He was unable to tear his eyes away until he lost sight of Bastian when he crested a small hill and started down the other side. He didn't blink once, unwilling to let the moisture that formed in his eyes to fall.

Taking a deep breath he gathered his packs. Well, he tried to gather his packs, but they were so heavy he couldn't lift them past his knees. Looking up, he saw Sir Balkan and Abadon with their packs hanging over their shoulders like they weighed nothing. Of course, they were both grown men and both much larger than Roland but still, Roland felt like a ninety pound weakling.

Abadon walked over. He stopped beside Roland and waved a glowing blue hand over Roland's packs, then turned and walked away.

Confused for a moment, Roland just stood there. Then he remembered Abadon was usually performing some kind of magic when he waved that marked hand around. Maybe Abadon just did something to his packs?

Leaning down, he grabbed a handle and lifted. He was expecting the pack to still be incredibly heavy, and was unprepared for it to be light as a feather. The force he applied lifting it caused him to stumble backwards, and he landed on his butt in the sand.

He heard someone snicker behind him. "Very funny," he said to no one in particular. Rising up, he easily lifted both packs and slung them each over a shoulder.

His curiosity about Abadon grew. Where did he come from? What was he exactly? How did he come to serve Eltanin? What about those markings? What did they mean? Sometime on this journey, he hoped to get answers.

He took exactly three steps when Sir Balkan barked at him.

"Cover your face!"

Oh yeah, thought Roland, he forgot.

Quickly patting pockets, he realized he had nothing to use until Abadon waved a scarf in his face. Wrapping it around his nose and mouth, he followed the other two.

The centaurs seemed to be content to follow and not lead this time. Turning to steal a quick peak, Roland saw they had something wrapped over their noses and mouths as well. A second glance showed Roland they had parted their long lower manes and crisscrossed it around their faces and tied it behind their heads. Gross! The thought of all that hair over their nose and mouth made Roland gag. He hated having hair in his mouth. The odd time he would find a hair in his meal he would run to the bathroom gagging and spitting.

He desperately tried to think of something else because he could feel bile rising up into his throat.

He started jogging to catch up to the other two, tucking himself in behind. He focused his eyes on the desert floor, trying to follow

Abadon's footsteps. Stretching his legs as far as he could wasn't enough to step in the footprints Abadon left in the sand. In fact, Roland had to take almost two steps between each one step that Abadon took. Man that guy had a big stride, Roland thought, hair situation forgotten.

They walked for quite some time, the wavering desert heat began taking its toll, even though it was evening. They were coated head to toe in dust, sweaty and thirsty. The only one who seemed to escape the heat was Abadon. He looked as cool as a cucumber. The dust didn't stick to his skin or his clothes. Roland wondered how he was managing that when… "Oof".

Sir Balkan had just taken a drink out of his water skin and Roland walked right into his back, sending the knight stumbling ahead. Turning, he glared at Roland a second before handing the water skin over to him, connecting with Roland's solar plexus. Roland expelled another oof.

Roland refused to bend over to catch his breath. He wasn't going to show how much that hurt, so he took a couple deep breaths, put the water skin to his mouth and took a long swallow. He tried to put lots of backwash in it in retaliation, before leaning forward to hand it back to Sir Balkan.

They trudged along for what seemed like ages. Roland figured they only had another hour or so before the pink sun went down and the black one rose. He wasn't sure he wanted to be walking around out here when that happened. He started thinking of home where the desert sands contained scorpions, poisonous snakes and all manner of other creepy crawly things just waiting for night to fall. Roland wasn't fond of insects and bugs. In fact, just thinking of it caused him to shiver. He scanned the desert floor as though all of those things were going to spring up suddenly out of their sandy hiding places and attack. Whoa, must change gears here, thought Roland. Think happy thoughts, he told himself, think football, think camping, think hanging out with his buddies, just, think about anything but creepy crawly things.

Before he could focus on anything else, sudden sandstorms sprung up around them, small swirling funnels that blasted sand in their faces, peppering any exposed skin painfully. Each grain of sand had enough force it felt like being shot with a tiny bullet. Roland covered his eyes with his hands, trying to peak between his fingers to see what was going on. They had all stopped walking, blinded by the impact of the tiny grains. He quickly closed his eyes again because even the tiniest opening was enough of an invitation for the granules to try to blast their way in.

When the swirling sand finally ceased, Roland slowly lowered his hands. Looking around, he was shocked to see they were surrounded by ten creatures made out of continuously swirling, twisting sand, like mini tornadoes. Looking closer, he could see separate swirls stuck out to form arms, legs and hands. There were no facial features nor any image of clothing discernable, just sand particles. Roland had no idea where they had come from. It was like they just sprung up from the ground. Looking between Abadon and Sir Balkan, he saw one of the creatures raise a swirling hand to point a spinning finger at the ground in front of it.

Abadon tilted his head down at Sir Balkan and Sir Balkan give a small nod. Together they stepped forward and promptly disappeared into the sand. It was as though they had stepped into water. One minute they were there, the next minute they were gone, swallowed by the unforgiving desert.

That same creature turned its featureless face to Roland and the centaurs and again pointed. They were to follow. The centaurs pawed at the ground and then King Tartae stepped forward. He too fell in, disappearing under the soft red pebbles. Pentally and

Roland looked at each other. Roland didn't see they had much choice, considering the circle of creatures surrounding them. He thought they were getting closer, tightening their ranks, eliminating any chance of escape. But escape to where? Roland thought. There was nowhere to go. There was nowhere to hide. Seeing those same thoughts reflected in Pentally's eyes, they made an unspoken agreement and stepped forward together.

21

Enter At Your Own Risk

Roland was thankful something was tied over his nose and mouth. He and Pentally were flying down a spinning tunnel of sand. The speed they travelled did not allow for them to have any control, and they spiraled downwards like riding a wild, crazy water slide. Bits of sand connected and tore at exposed skin. His forehead felt as though it was being shredded like cheese. He squeezed his eyes as tight as he could to try and protect them.

Travelling at that speed, unable to see where he was going, made his stomach turn. And then he was airborne, soaring like an eagle. He flayed his arms helplessly and grunted when he hit the hard sand packed bottom with a thump. His momentum was great enough that he slid five feet before coming to a stop. He felt someone's hands under his armpits, lifting him to his feet. Pulling the cover down from his nose and mouth, he wiped the collection of sand out of his eyes and shook out of his hair. He looked up to see Abadon standing over him. He glanced around quickly to see how Pentally faired, and saw his father helping him to his feet, brushing the sand off his back.

And for the briefest of seconds Roland froze as a thought occurred to him. "Oh no," he said frantically, "Finch!"

Pulling aside his jacket, his pocket was almost bursting with sand. Taking his jacket off quickly but carefully with shaking hands, Roland knelt down and carefully dumped it out slowly. Finch's lifeless little body came last, hitting the top of the small sand pile only to roll off and lay still.

Looking up in anguish, Roland pleaded, "Help him Abadon, please, can you help him?"

Leaning over Roland's shoulder, Abadon's white markings on his face and hands began to glow with that ethereal blue light. Reaching down, he gently picked up the little fire sprite. Finch lay in Abadon's large dark hand like a rag doll, unmoving and lifeless. Whispering gently, Abadon put his other hand over the top, raising the cupped hands to his mouth. The markings flared brightly and Abadon blew lightly between his thumbs. Lowering his hands, he slowly removed the top one. Finch still lay quietly, looking so small and helpless that it was heartbreaking.

Roland felt tears gather in his eyes as he looked up into Abadon's face. Abadon met Roland's anguished eyes and held his index finger up just before Roland could ask if Finch was going to be okay. Breathless, Roland's eyes returned to the lifeless little body, willing the sprite to breathe. Just when hope was almost gone, the little guy started sputtering and coughing. Particles of sand billowed out of his little mouth, peppering Abadon's palm. It was the greatest sound Roland had ever heard!

"He's okay," Roland yelled. "He's okay Abadon! Thank you, thank you, thank you," Roland cried, flinging himself at Abadon, wrapping his arms around his waist, hugging tightly.

A tiny little voice called, "Wollaan... Wollaan?"

Letting go of Abadon, Roland rubbed quickly at his cheeks, embarrassed at his emotion. Leaning over Abadon's hand, Roland answered, "I am right here Finch. How are you doing little buddy?"

Standing up on Abadon's hand, the little sprite shook himself like a wet dog, spraying sand all over. Flapping his wings, he rose up into the air, fluttered in Abadon's face for a second before reaching out and grasping either side of the large man's nose with his little nubby hands. Before Abadon could wave him away, Finch gave Abadon a loud, noisy kiss on the end of his nose. Hiking up his little red and yellow polka dot pants, he gave a little twirl in the air, before flying to Roland to land on his favorite perch, Roland's shoulder. Leaning closely he tucked himself in and stroked Roland's neck, vibrating in happiness.

Abadon reached up and wiped the kiss off his nose, a disgusted look on his face. That small gesture and the look on Abadon's face had an unexpected reaction. Every single one of them burst out laughing. They laughed until tears rolled. Even Finch squeaked happily, not realizing they were laughing at him.

When they got themselves together, Abadon cleared his throat. "Hide, fire sprite must. Coming they are. Jacket you need Roland."

Roland picked up his precious jacket and shook it out. Putting it back on, he opened the pocket and told Finch he needed to hide. Finch instantly dove into the pocket.

They were all filthy. He had sand in places he never ever wanted to have sand again! He was glad no one else had been hurt. Before they could take a single step, the creatures were there, circling them again. That was when Roland realized they were in a chamber. He was so wrapped up in Finch, he hadn't even taken stock of where they were.

Directing them as before, a creature pointed to a single doorway, the message clear. Move!

Sir Balkan went first, then the centaurs, then Abadon, and finally Roland, who followed quietly. He was wondering why they didn't take a stand here in this room and fight to escape. They still had their bags and weapons after all. He decided if fighting was an option, Sir Balkan would have pulled his sword, Abadon his staff and the battle would have been underway. For whatever reason, they were allowing themselves to be captured. Roland just had to trust that Sir Balkan knew what he was doing.

They followed a maze of tunnels for what seemed like forever. Not a word was spoken by anyone. The walls were dense and solid, like being inside a cave. He suddenly remembered his dragon tear, and he quickly checked his pants pocket for it, having transferred it there for safekeeping after their battle with the Goren. Mentally sighing in relief when his fingers touched it, he rubbed it slowly, its smoothness somehow comforting.

They eventually came to a large room that was obviously a jail with a large open centre, circled by approximately thirty cells. They were built into hard packed sand and each had its own door with heavy metal bars. Hearing movement, Roland realized with horror that some of the cells already had occupants.

Their packs and weapons, Sir Balkan's sword and the centaur's bows and arrows, armor and cloaks, were stripped away and dropped in the middle of the room. The sand waifs did not seem concerned their prisoners would be retrieving them, however, Roland was confused as to why the sand waifs left Sir Balkan with his armor but took the centaurs'. Maybe it was because the centaurs were much larger and potentially more dangerous? Mentally shrugging it off, he needed to focus on more important things. Like, what the heck were they gonna do now?

Two cell doors were opened and the centaurs were directed into one, while Roland, Sir Balkan and Abadon were shoved into the cell beside. Four sand creatures remained on guard, while the rest swirled away.

"I hope this was part of your plan to get us into the city Balkan," growled King Tartae from next door.

"Entering undetected would have been best case scenario," replied Sir Balkan, "but since no one knows where the entrances are, unless *you* could see the tunnel through the sand," he said sarcastically, "getting captured by the sand waifs is the only way in."

"You mean we had to be captured and thrown into jail?" asked Roland, feeling relieved that it was all part of the plan.

"Isn't that what I just said?" Sir Balkan replied without looking at Roland.

"Captured for a reason we were. Need to be here we did. Plan now we must make." Abadon stated.

"Yes, and no one is going to like what that is," Sir Balkan said with a dark undertone to his voice.

"What? What do you mean?" Roland asked anxiously. He was getting awful tired of feeling like a little kid trying to figure out what the grown-ups were saying.

It appeared King Tartae felt the same when he said, "We need to know what we are up against, what to expect and what is going on Balkan and Abadon, so someone start talking!"

Sir Balkan began pacing in the cell, his armor making grinding noises from the sand trapped in the crevasses. "The sand waifs hunt during the day, but they do not hunt for themselves. No one knows what they themselves actually eat. You see, they gather whatever they find while roaming the desert, like they just did with us. During the day, they are the sand waifs we saw. They cannot be destroyed then for they are nothing but air and sand. However, at night they become solid forms, solid like us, with flesh, blood and bone. They gather the food," he hesitated, "they gather the food for a creature called the Sulandow. We were captured to be its food."

As soon as Roland heard the name Sulandow, the scroll popped into his head. It was beginning to make sense! The scroll said the sands of time flow through the glass.

326

Sand! The sand city! Search for a cave deep underground was another clue. Here they were! It also said, beware the Sulandow who prowls around. The Sulandow! The clues fell into place. The artifact they were looking for was being protected by the Sulandow! In order to retrieve the artifact, they were going to have to become its meal, like lambs being let to slaughter!

22

Share the Secret

Roland tugged frantically on Abadon's sleeve. When Abadon turned to him, he excitedly whispered all this to him.

"Indeed, sense it all makes," Abadon said nodding his head in agreement. "Others now we will tell."

And with that, Abadon did tell. Speaking softly and quietly he told the story. He told them about the six artifacts and why they were so important to find. He told them about the scrolls and the clues they provided and what the first scroll said. He told them about the stolen Timekeeper, the eclipse and Rahm's plan. He told them about Roland seeing the Spirit Dragons, and how he was the one from the ancient prophecy, the one who could save the realm. He was very clever though, thought Roland, because the only thing he didn't tell them, that he kept secret, was the fact that Roland held a part of Chelios's spirit within him.

King Tartae grumbled that he didn't understand why they weren't told this in the first place, but the king had a new understanding of Roland's purpose and role.

"Abadon," Roland whispered, "if the centaurs didn't know any of this, why did they come along in the first place? And Sir Balkan? Why did he come?"

"Quest to defeat Rahm, they did know. Save centaur herd is king's role. Sir Balkan along to protect you." Abadon answered simply, as though no other reasoning was needed. Thinking on it, Roland realized there wasn't.

"What do we do now?" Pentally's voice came through the bars of the other cell. Roland was shocked to hear him speak for the first time.

"We have five other artifacts to find and just over three weeks to do it. We cannot afford to waste any time. We need to get the first one tonight and get out of here. If the artifact is being guarded by the Sulandow, as Roland thinks, then we need to get to the Sulandow to find it. To do that, we need to become its next meal." Sir Balkan told them.

"How sure is the boy the artifact is being guarded by this thing? We are putting our lives on the line. He better not just think, he better know!" King Tartae stated in his usual demanding tone.

"Believe I do, right Roland is. Stay here and wait for us you can." Abadon responded calmly.

King Tartae blustered, "I am not waiting behind. I just wanted to be sure that he knows what he's talking about and not leading us all on a wild chase."

"Alright then, everyone is in?" Sir Balkan asked.

"How do we make sure we are its next meal?" Roland asked with trepidation. He had a very bad feeling about this.

Abadon turned to Sir Balkan with a raised eyebrow. Sir Balkan was the expert on these creatures and would have to come up with a plan. He knew it too, and started pacing in the cell. He turned suddenly and snapped his fingers.

"The sand waifs are very sensitive to noise. If we make a lot of noise, I think that would be enough for them to want to get rid of us tonight. If we raise a ruckus, it would make their meal choice easy."

"Please Abadon, take me with you?" a small, whispery voice spoke from one of the other cells.

Abadon turned so fast, his ear chains jingled and chimed.

"Identify yourself!" he commanded, his markings beginning to glow.

Roland took a step back. He had never seen Abadon in such a state before.

Turning to the bars, Roland grasped them, squeezing his head between two of them, trying to see into the surrounding cells. He could pick out nothing. They were too dark.

"It's me, Kentor. I have been in here for a long time, days and days and days. I don't want to be eaten. Please take me with you," the voice pleaded.

"You!" exclaimed Abadon. "You were banished from Katori! You are the traitor that stole the Timekeeper! You are the reason we are facing the end of our realm. You are getting what you deserve!" Abadon's loud, angry voice echoed off the walls, "what you deserve, what you deserve, what you deserve."

"I didn't steal the Timekeeper, I swear!" the voice shouted back. "I didn't do it. I don't want to see the realm destroyed. It's my home too. I know I made mistakes Abadon, but please, let me prove it to you. Let me prove my innocence. Let me help you!"

Roland poked at Abadon's shoulder to get his attention. The warlock turned so fast that Roland stumbled backward. "What is it?" he shouted in Roland's face.

Wringing his hands together, Abadon's angry countenance made Roland nervous. "The spirit dragons mentioned Kentor, Abadon. They said he would be with us on this quest. They didn't know if this would be a good thing or a bad thing, but they saw him coming along." Roland shrugged. "I just thought you should know that."

Abadon put his hands on his hips glaring at the wall behind Roland's head. Roland didn't like this Abadon. He was scary when he was angry.

"Unexpected. Not good is this. Sir Balkan, with him we should do what?"

"I don't think we have a choice Abadon. I think we have to bring him with us. He knows too much now. We can't risk him sharing what he has heard, of him telling anyone of our plan. It would be all over, right here, right now."

Abadon rubbed his bald head, clearly agitated and frustrated with the current situation. "Others hear?" he asked as the thought dawned on him.

"I don't think so," said Sir Balkan. "Only Kentor would have the ability to hear us. We spoke very quietly."

"Right," Abadon said with obvious relief. "No choice, bring him we must. Decide later we will, escape first."

"Yeah, we'll figure out what to do with him later." Sir Balkan confirmed.

Abadon walked over to the cell door and leaned close to the wall that separated them from the centaurs. Roland heard whispering. He assumed Abadon was telling the centaurs what they had just discussed. King Tartae must have agreed with all that was said because Roland didn't hear any furious whispering in reply.

Addressing Kentor, Abadon called out, "agreed it is. Come with us you will. Trust you we do not. Betray us and die!"

Roland gasped.

"I understand." the voice replied gratefully.

23

Kentor

oland wanted to ask more questions about Kentor but realized it would have to wait. They had more pressing matters to deal with first.

Finch started squirming in Roland's pocket. Opening his jacket, he whispered, "You can't come out yet Finch. It's too dangerous. You have to stay in there okay?"

The little sprite whimpered, but nodded his head and sank back down into Roland's pocket. Roland figured he was probably hungry, but he had nothing to give him to eat right now. All their food was in the packs, on the other side of the bars! That thought made Roland whisper to Abadon again.

"What about the scrolls Abadon. They are sitting right on top in the knapsack! What are we gonna do about them?"

"Destroy them I will."

"Okay, yeah, that's a good idea. We don't want the sand waifs to get their hands on them."

Sir Balkan announced the black sun was rising. It was time to make some noise!

Abadon, Roland and Sir Balkan began yelling and shouting while the centaurs kicked at the walls and bars with their hooves, shouting as well. Kentor was banging the bars and letting off loud vibrating growls interspersed with roars that shook the room. Roland wondered exactly what kind of creature Kentor was. Were they letting a gigantic, man eating lion join them or some equally scary, hideous thing? Whatever it was, it sounded big and it sounded dangerous, very dangerous.

They carried on yelling and banging until Roland's voice became hoarse and his hands hurt from hitting the bars. They could only hope they achieved their goal when the sand waifs suddenly swirled back into the room.

The four guards had not moved or made a sound the whole time. In fact, Roland had forgotten they were even there. Panic set in. What if they heard their plans? At the very least, they would have heard the conversation between Kentor and Abadon. Were they done for?

Roland tapped Abadon on the shoulder to get his attention and pointed at the four guards. Abadon shook his head, indicating they were not a concern. When Roland frowned in confusion, Abadon leaned over. "Speak they cannot. Hear, they cannot."

"Well if they can't hear, why did we just make all that noise?"

"Because they can feel all the vibrations we are making and they don't like that." Sir Balkan explained.

They not only continued their banging and shouting, but jacked the volume even higher to ensure they were the ones chosen for the Sulandow's supper.

Roland thought they had succeeded when three guards approached, but then was not so sure when the guards stopped just before opening their cell doors. What were they doing? Why weren't they opening the doors? Come on, come on, open the doors, you whirling pieces of sand paper, he thought to himself in frustration.

The two sand waifs standing outside the cell bars began to waver and their swirling sand began to slow. Roland remembered Sir Balkan saying something about them having a different form at night than they do during the day. He watched in fascination to see what they would turn into.

Roland scrutinized them through the bars as the sand stopped swirling and their alternate form was revealed. Roland wished he hadn't been so curious. They were disgusting!

Their skin retained the color and texture of the sand, however, their arms, legs and bare chests were cover with hundreds of growths.

They had hairless lumpy scalps and black gooey pockets of liquid for eyes. There was no nose, ears or mouth. Their entire face was covered in small bulging lumps. They were downright repugnant. They were much better to look at when they were swirling piles of sand!

Once the change was complete, the hideous guards opened the doors to the three noisy cells. It had worked. They were going to the Sulandow. Dread filled Roland's stomach.

The guards indicated they should come out of the cells. The centaurs emerged from theirs first. Roland could see King Tartae flexing fisted hands, and hoped he could control himself until they got where they needed to go. They would never find the Sulandow on their own, so starting a fight here and now would be a very bad idea. After all, they were in a city. That meant thousands, maybe hundreds of thousands of these creatures wondering around. No, this was the only way they were going to get that artifact. They had to be led to the Sulandow.

Roland, Abadon and Sir Balkan walked out when their door was opened. No one else but Roland noticed a brief blue glow from Abadon's hand as it hovered over the knapsack for the briefest of moments. The scrolls that had been sticking out in all directions disappeared. Abadon discretely tucked his hands behind his back and stood still as a stature.

And then the third cell, containing the mysterious Kentor, was opened. Roland got the shock of his life. It wasn't a lion or any kind of gruesome creature that made all the roaring and growling sounds. It was a dragon!

Roland stared transfixed at the young dragon as it emerged from the confines of the dark, dingy cell. He came out like a terrified animal. His belly almost touched the ground, his tail was tucked between his legs and he crawled forward, stopping in front of

Abadon, where the dragon hung his head low.

"Thank you master for letting me come with you," he said.

That was when Roland realized how much the dragon must have gone through all this time here in the dark, dungeon like cell. He had to have been wondering every time the sand waifs came if it was his turn to be some creature's supper. How awful! The dragon's pathetic countenance tugged at Roland's soft heart. He tried to stop himself from feeling sorry for it, as it was after all, a thief. Not just any thief either, but the one who stole the Timekeeper, hence the reason they were all in this mess! But he just kept imagining, night after night, the fear it must have felt over and over again, of being fed to a monster. He shivered.

Abadon stared down at the dragon's bent head and only made one sound, "Hmmmm."

The guards gathered behind them and Roland felt something sharp pressing into his back, sending him forward. He had no more time to think about the young dragon. He couldn't even tell what color it was because the lighting was so dim. He gave his head a slight shake. He needed to focus on the scroll and the words it had revealed. He felt so scared that for a moment he couldn't remember one single word. He had to do better than that. The words on that scroll would be what would save their lives. The panic rose so quickly it felt like a living thing trying to claw its way out of his throat. He swallowed it down. Focus, he told himself. Focus!

The scroll came back to him as he began to walk the maze of halls, passing many open caves. The words played in his head as he gazed into the caves as they passed by. Each cave seemed to be filled with the transformed creatures and they all looked identical. There were no distinguishing features among any of them. It was like they all came from the same mold. Some caves had fires going but

Roland wasn't sure what for. He didn't see anyone cooking or eating anything. Roland didn't see any furniture either, of any kind, and all the rooms seemed to be just that. An open room with only one way in and one way out.

Forcing his mind back to the words of the scroll, he repeated it over and over again, like a mantra. He paid special attention to the parts of the scroll he hadn't figured out yet.

They walked and walked and walked. Wherever this Sulandow was, it was obviously a long way from the city. This made sense, as they wouldn't want to keep a dangerous creature like that close to the general population. This was good, he decided, because when they were ready to escape, they wouldn't have to worry about trying to evade thousands of those creatures hunting them in the middle of the city. Escape would, hopefully, be easier and quicker this way.

They finally stopped at the only doors, beside their cell doors, they had come across. They must be here!

Roland felt his body break out into a cold clammy sweat. This was it. They were either going to die here, eaten by some horrible monster, or they were going to triumph, retrieve the first artifact and escape. Roland prayed for the latter.

One of the guards stepped forward with a key in its lumpy, wart covered hand. He inserted it into the lock. Roland couldn't seem to take his eyes off the grotesque misshapen hand. The sound of the key echoed in the silence. It was both hollow and desperate.

Two waifs stepped forward to pull the doors open. They were then shoved into the waiting darkness of the room beyond. The door was slammed closed, leaving them all in complete and utter inky blackness. The lock clicked again ominously. They were locked in!

24

A Royal Sacrifice

Roland could hear a harsh breathing sound along with a scrabbling, scratching noise somewhere in front of him. He wished desperately for his pack of supplies, or for any of them to have even one pack. He was sure there would have been something in there they could have used as a weapon, or would have at least provided some light. Standing there in the dark, Roland felt like a giant dart board. The thing could attack them one at a time and they would never see it coming. His heart sank. It was over. They were done. All that remained was the unbearable tension of waiting to become supper.

A dim light began to glow, getting brighter every second. Roland rubbed his eyes. Yes, it was real! It was Abadon. He had some kind of torch in his hand. It was very small though. Small wings fluttered. Roland realized it was one of the fireflies from the forest, perched on the end of Abadon's staff. Abadon had his staff? A small surge of hope filled Roland. The light the firefly gave off wasn't bright, but it was better than nothing. The group quickly formed a circle, then turned to face outward, as each searched the shadows, carefully looking for the deadly creature.

"There! I see it," Roland whispered. "It's directly in front of me. Do you see it? It's the black shadow there on the wall," he said pointing. He heard Pentally shifting restlessly.

A gigantic black silhouette stood where Roland indicated. It was still and silent. Its shadow, from what they could discern in the dim light, was like a bat or moth like creature. It was hard to tell which. Roland could see wings with long sharp velociraptor like claws rising up behind a large head with wide pointed ears. Standing on long thin hind legs, it was about twelve feet tall. A thick chest and skinny arms, each ending in one enormous talon was all Roland could make out in the light. He was sure the only reason it hadn't attacked yet was because of Abadon's light. He could hear a splatting sound, like water dripping from the ceiling. Just then, Abadon sent the firefly forward and Roland saw the splatting sound was saliva dripping from sharp pointed teeth onto the floor. The creature shrank back from the light with a snarl, bringing one wing up protectively.

The smell in the room was enough to gag them. It was the smell of dead things, some old dead and some newly dead and some decomposing dead. Pentally was standing beside Roland and when he moved, Roland could hear crunching sounds under Pentally's hooves. He was pretty sure it was bones.

"I need some kind of weapon Abadon. Can you help me out here?" Sir Balkan whispered. Abadon's markings began to glow and he whispered strange words. His markings got brighter and brighter until there was a flash of blue light. The Sulandow shrieked at them in anger.

"That's better," Sir Balkan said sounding satisfied. Roland heard the telltale sound of steel sliding out of its holder, and knew that Sir Balkan had drawn his sword.

The magical effort for Abadon must have been great however, because Roland saw his shoulders slump and heard a quiet groan from the warlock.

"Are you okay Abadon?" he whispered.

"Fine I will be," Abadon answered slowly. "Very difficult it is to gather magic. So little in realm. Moment to rest I need. Much it takes now to do even small magic."

"Move into the middle of the circle Abadon. We will protect you for as long as we can," Sir Balkan instructed.

"No, need me you do. Fine I will be. Watch now. Closer it comes."

The creature was moving silently, stalking them like a black panther, yellow glowing eyes stared. It circled the group, searching for either an opening to attack or for the weakest link. Roland had never been so scared. A gurgling sound was coming out of its mouth, interspersed with sharp chirping noises.

Right then, Roland realized what it was doing. It was applying echo location. It was sending out signals to have them bounce back in order to know where they were.

Before Roland could share that information with the rest though, it attacked. King Tartae was the target and Roland heard him yell as the creature had seized the opportunity when the King's attention was on Abadon.

King Tartae was positioned at the other end of the circle behind Roland, his back end so close that Tartac's tail whipped Roland across the back of his head. Turning, Roland watched in horror as the shadow creature swung its left wing and claw at the centaur king, catching him across the chest. It quickly followed with a swing of its right wing before King Tartae could bring his arms up to block. Its movements were so quick and so silent, the centaur was unprepared. Blood blossomed from two deep cuts across his chest.

Sir Balkan stepped forward and thrust his sword in the creature while it was bringing its wing back, preparing for another brutal swipe. The sword was deadly and accurate, striking directly at the heart of the creature, sliding effortlessly right up to the hilt. Sir Balkan pulled the sword free as Pentally screamed for his father, shifting to catch him as King Tartae's front legs gave out. He went down in a bizarre resemblance of a bow. Roland could hear him gasping for breath. A thick rattling sound echoed in the silence.

Roland couldn't just stand there. He went over to Tartae, but was shoved out of the way by Abadon, as the creature rose above them to attack again.

Stumbling backward, Roland stared up at the creature. How was it possible? Sir Balkan had stabbed it right in the heart. It should be dead!

Its left wing swooped in, razor sharp claws having only one deadly purpose.

"Get down!" Abadon shouted at them.

Roland hit the floor. Pentally was kneeling down beside his father, leaning over him protectively, making himself as small a target as possible.

Roland could hear Pentally whispering to his father that he was going to be okay, that everything was going to be okay. Roland figured he was saying it more to himself than to his father.

A great rush of air followed the swing, but the Sulandow lost its balance from putting such effort into swinging and not making any contact, that it stumbled backward before quickly righting itself. Its chirping noises became more frantic. Roland stared, scared witless as the creature lowered its head.

Oh no, he thought, it was searching for the king. It knew he was wounded. It was going to go for the weakest prey. They had nowhere to take King Tartae to protect him. This creature could play with them for days, patiently stalking and killing them one at a time. They had no defense as Sir Balkan's sword was useless.

"Abadon," Roland shouted, "it's going to go for the King again!"

Roland jumped over the back of the downed centaur, and stood directly in front of the centaur king and his son. Waving his arms wildly, he hoped to confuse it. Maybe, just maybe it would think that its prey wasn't wounded as badly as it thought.

The creature paused.

Behind him King Tartae moaned, "Don't boy. Get out of the way. It will kill you! You must survive. You are the hope of our realm!"

King Tartae struggled to his feet.

Pentally gasped, "No father, no!"

All Roland knew was that one minute he was standing there and the next, he was airborne, thrown across the room. He hit the wall hard and slid down, winded. Sucking air in painfully, Roland realized King Tartae had thrown him out of the way. He felt a sharp pain in his lower leg below the knee, but it was quickly forgotten as all he could do now was watch what happened next.

King Tartae put his arm out to hold his precious son out of the way, and took a violent strike by the winged claws one more time. His decision was one he made for the Realm of Abraxas, for his precious son, and for the boy Roland. It was the greatest of sacrifices.

This time he went down and didn't get back up.

"NOOOOO," screamed Pentally, readying himself to charge at the shadow. His howl of pain and desperation sent shivers up Roland's spine. Rearing up, his hooves pawed at the air and his hands formed into fists. Roland rose up off the floor, pain slicing through his leg. Ignoring it as best he could, he hobbled as fast as he could, focused on the young centaur, who was going to be the next to be destroyed by the knife-like claws of the monstrous creature.

Each and every one of them, even the dragon, rushed in to help the young centaur. But this time, the shadow creature didn't use its wings, and they were unprepared when its tail whipped around catching Pentally in the shoulder and Roland across his upper arm, cutting deep down through the muscle, almost to the bone.

Sir Balkan had tried to block the tail with his sword, but the tail sailed right through it, as though it wasn't even there. No wonder it didn't die when Sir Balkan stabbed it. His sword was completely useless. The direness of the situation hit Roland like a freight train. They had no way to defend themselves. Nothing to save them, nothing to fight it, nothing to defeat it! Holding his blood soaked arm, his stomach sank.

Abadon stepped forward, sending the firefly into its face. It let out a piercing shriek and stepped back. The words of the scroll flashed through Roland's mind like a slideshow. *"Blades of steel only cause strife,"* and the next line, *"Pierce of sound may save one's life"*. Pierce of sound, pierce of sound, the words clambered around in Roland's head. He felt like the answer was right there in front of him, but he couldn't seem to grasp hold of it.

The firefly hovered in front of the creature, keeping it back, but it wouldn't stay back forever. It would attack again and again and again, until they all lay bleeding and dying, or dead.

The words stopped spinning in his head. "Abadon!" he shouted, "Abadon, whistle! Whistle as loud and as long as you can!"

Abadon looked over his shoulder at Roland.

"Now, do it now!" Roland screamed. "As long as you can!"

Abadon turned back to the Sulandow, took a deep breath and let out a piercing whistle. The creature instantly screamed back. Between the two of them, it was so sharp, that Pentally, Sir Balkan and Roland covered their ears. The Sulandow began stumbling backward as though in pain, screaming back at Abadon, its wings waving uncontrollably.

Abadon held the whistle as long as he could but his shoulders began to slump as the air was expelled from his lungs.

"It's working," Roland yelled, "keep going!"

The creature had stopped his own screaming and was thrashing around, turning in circles like it wanted to escape the noise, but had nowhere to go.

Roland worried Abadon would run out of air before the creature could be destroyed. He could hear the strain in the whistle as his air supply was tapering off. The whistle started to wobble as the warlock struggled desperately to continue blowing air that was no longer there. A dreadful silence filled the room before Abadon dragged deep gulps of air back into his lungs.

Panic set in. "Someone whistle!" Roland screamed. "Come on, come on! I can't! I can't whistle! Sir Balkan, start whistling," he shouted desperately. "Hurry before it attacks again!" Sulandow had stopped its frantic movements and was now shaking its head as though to clear it.

As he watched the creature gather itself up, stretching on its hind legs, Roland knew time was quickly running out and they were going to be late. It was preparing for another attack!

And then a new piercing sound started. This one even louder and higher pitched than Abadon's, grew in strength by the second.

Whipping his head around in the direction of the sound, Roland saw the dragon, his head thrown back like a wolf howling at the moon, releasing the piercing whistle. Strong and true, the whistling grew in volume and Roland had to cover his ears again, the pain on his own eardrums triple what Abadon's had been. It was almost unbearable, his eardrums felt like they were about to burst.

The creature instantly resumed screaming and this time, it fell to the floor, writhing like never before, until only short jerky movements of its body remained, and then there was no movement at all.

And still the dragon whistled.

Abadon moved over to touch Kentor on his shoulder, getting his attention. Kentor stopped his piercing whistle, dragging in great pockets of air, his body sagging onto the floor.

The only sound in the room was the sobbing of Pentally. He was kneeling beside his father's lifeless body. The King of the Overton Centaurs had made the greatest sacrifice of all. Himself.

They gathered around, sharing in the grief, each lost in their own thoughts. Roland noticed, with surprise, a pounding pain in his right arm and left leg. He remembered his leg hurting earlier after hitting the wall, but he had completely forgotten about it. Stepping to the side with a hobble, he examined his wounds.

Looking at his leg first, he felt faint when he saw his pant leg, below the knee, soaked in blood. Something white was sticking straight out of a tear in the material. Shock set in. He just stared at it. Feeling a touch on his shoulder, he raised his head to see Sir Balkan step in front of him. His gaze was down, looking at the foreign object sticking out.

Sir Balkan hadn't escaped the battle with the Sulandow either. He had a wide gash that very nearly took off a chunk of his ear before running diagonally across his cheek to the corner of his mouth. The flesh of his ear hung over like a flap and the blood ran unchecked down the side of his face, down his neck, disappearing under his black tunic.

"That needs to come out," he told Roland, indicating the white object.

Roland winced. That was gonna hurt!

"What is it?" he asked very calmly, still in shock.

"Are you sure you want to know?" Sir Balkan's tone said he would be better off not knowing.

"Yeah."

"It's bone."

"Bone?"

"Yes, bone."

"You mean my bone?"

"No, someone else's."

"Oh."

"You might want to sit down so I can deal with this."

"Okay."

Sitting down, Roland cradled his left arm where the blood still flowed from the deep gash.

"On the count of three, I am going to pull it out. Ready?" Roland shook his head no.

Sir Balkan ignored him and started counting. "One, two...." And Sir Balkan yanked it out.

Roland screamed with the fierce rush of fiery pain that travelled up his leg to his brain. What the? That wasn't a three count, it was only two! The vision around his eyes turned a fuzzy grey and then to black.

He fell backward in a dead faint.

That's for the best Sir Balkan realized. Now he could wrap it tight to stop the bleeding. It was all he could do for now. They had to get out of there first before it could be dealt with properly. Kid had some heart, though. That was the second time he had seen him step in front of death to try and save someone else. The first time was when Roland saved him from the rock lion.

Coming to, Roland groaned, raising himself up off the cold, bone littered floor to a sitting position.

"That hurt!"

"Yep." The knight replied.

"You didn't pull on three."

"Nope."

"Did you get it out?"

"Yep."

"Is it gonna be okay?"

"Uh huh."

"Are you okay?"

"Uh huh."

Roland saw the knight had torn off the bottom of his tunic to wrap around his leg.

"Uh, thanks for fixing my leg."

"Uh huh."

"You talk too much you know," Roland said, eyeing the knight's handy work on his leg.

"Uh huh."

The knight walked away. Roland's leg throbbed unbearably, but Roland was going to have to shove the pain down deep inside. Giving his head a slight shake, he tried to clear the remaining grey film from his vision.

Rising up off the crunchy floor, Roland winced. This quest was not done yet!

25

Blood of the Innocent Magic

King Tartae had been carefully lifted up and was now draped over the back of the dragon. The extra weight did not seem to be too much for him. Roland was relieved. He had not wanted to see this proud warrior king left down here in this darkness, alone forever. Pentally stood beside the dragon, holding onto his father's limp hand.

Abadon took charge. He also knew they were not finished here yet. They must retrieve the artifact.

"Pentally and Kentor stay. Guard the entrance. Go retrieve the artifact we must. Return we will."

Kentor nodded his understanding. Pentally had no reaction, so deep was he in his grief that Roland didn't think he even heard.

Turning with the dim firefly leading the way, Abadon walked in the direction where Roland had first spotted the creature. Waving Sir Balkan and Roland to follow, Abadon moved slowly to the back of the cave. The light was just not bright enough to allow them to see the wall clearly. In fact, the firefly's light was growing dimmer by the second.

"We need more light," Sir Balkan declared.

"I cannot. No power left. Have to do, this will," Abadon said, almost touching the firefly to the wall to see.

"Hey, wait a minute," said Roland, "I have an idea."

Opening his jacket, he called, "Finch, hey Finch, buddy, I need you to come out now."

Finch flew out of Roland's pocket, looking around in fright. "It's okay Finch, it's okay.

Nothing is gonna hurt you. Listen Finch. I need to know if you can make some light for us. Like a bright fire. Can you do that?"

Babbling excitedly in reply, Finch hovered for a moment before going quiet. And then all his tail ribbons burst into a dazzling, fiery red. The streams of ribbons were so intense, it lit the whole room. Finch was like a miniature volcano, spewing ribbons of lava.

"That's awesome Finch, great job," Roland congratulated the sprite. "Keep it going as long as you can okay buddy? And stay with us."

Finch puffed out his little chest proudly, nodding his head enthusiastically.

"We could have used that little sh..," But Sir Balkan didn't get a chance to finish because Abadon interrupted quickly, knowing what word Sir Balkan was going to use, "Yes, but think of it no one did. You not think of sprite either."

"Hey you be nice to him!" Roland whirled around on Sir Balkan, taking offense at what the knight was going to call his little friend. "If it's anyone's fault, it's mine. I should have thought to use Finch earlier against the Sulandow. If I had, King Tartae...."

"Enough! Finish this we must. No one's fault. Done is done." Abadon commanded before telling Finch to move to the wall in front of them.

It didn't take long with Finch's bright firelight for Abadon to find a narrow channel set into the back wall.

A huge pile of bones was stacked in front of a narrow opening. Abadon and Sir Balkan began using their feet and hands to push the bones out of the way. Disturbing the bones made the air smell even fouler than before. Roland couldn't help it. He grabbed the collar of his shirt and hiked it up over his nose and mouth. He saw Finch pinching his little nose closed.

Once the opening was cleared, Abadon went first, having to turn sideways in order to enter. Roland went next. He could just fit through without turning, but his shoulders rubbed against the sides.

Sir Balkan tried to follow, but even turning sideways he couldn't fit. It was his armor. With no hesitation, the knight stripped off his shoulder, back and chest plates, laying them to the side. He then quickly followed after them, bringing only the sword Abadon had magically returned to him.

They travelled about ten feet when the tunnel widened enough that Abadon and Sir Balkan could face forward. Walking another twenty feet, the tunnel ended and they emerged into a small chamber.

Finch flew around the room trying to light it up, but thick black walls sucked the light into its pores, leaving only a spooky illumination.

The air smelled slightly better in here, having no rotting flesh or bones strewn about the floor to foul it up. Obviously the creature never entered this space.

There, in the centre of the room, was what they came for. A single, white, floating feather hovered above the middle of a black dusty pedestal.

Seriously, thought Roland in disgust, a feather? What in the heck were they going to do with that? Tickle Rahm to death? King Tartae had just given his life, and a son just lost his father... for a feather?

As though reading his thoughts, Abadon said quietly, "Powerful magic it has Roland. Make no judgements. Power comes in all forms."

"I sure hope so, because it all seems so pointless right now just for a feather." Roland replied with disgust.

They approached the pedestal and saw a hazy, black fog surrounding the feather. Flanking the pedestal, they climbed the four steps to the top.

They stood staring at the floating feather when Sir Balkan reached out for it. Quick as a snake, Abadon grabbed his wrist, stopping him.

"Touch it not Sir Balkan. Protected it is. Black magic it be. Kill you it will. Only Roland."

Roland's head snapped up. What? Him? How was he supposed to do that? He locked gazes with the warlock. Abadon only stared at him, waiting.

Taking a deep breath and letting it out slowly, Roland thought to himself. Okay, alright, well it had to come back to the scroll. Replaying the words quickly in his mind, he realized that Abadon was right. He did know how to do this! *Blood of the innocent magic shall pass.* That was the clue!

Looking down, he waved the other two aside. Sir Balkan hesitated, then followed when Abadon stepped down off the steps. Roland walked slowly around the pedestal until he found what he was looking for. A small semicircular dish protruding just below the lip of the pedestal at the back. Stepping closer he raised his left arm over the dish so that his hand was hanging down over the top. Removing his right hand from where it was clutching the deep gash on his arm, he watched as blood instantly began to run down his arm. The pain increased and a deep, pulsating throb matched with every beat of his heart.

Ignoring the pain as best he could, Roland let the blood run, dripping in steady drops off his fingers, splashing in the dish. It filled quickly, making little plopping sounds now. He waited until the pint-sized dish was full. Clapping his hand once again over the wound, he leaned back and whispered, "Blood of the innocent magic shall pass".

A white, marble basin materialized under the feather and the blood disappeared from the dish, only to reappear, pouring out of an invisible spout into the basin. The black fog began to sputter and hiss, smoke rising like water being thrown onto a fire.

When the basin was full, the fog sputtered one last time before collapsing away from the feather one strip at a time, like peeling a banana. Landing on the flat surface of the pedestal, the black fog formed long coils that slithered over the side of the basin, gliding away like black mamba snakes.

Shivering, Roland watched them until they vanished, disappearing into a small hole in the wall.

No longer surrounded by the black inky fog, the whiteness of the feather was so bright, so intense, Roland had to turn his head away.

Receiving a nod from Abadon to proceed, Roland very slowly and very carefully reached out to grasp the bottom of the feather. It was as long as his arm and had a surprising weight to it. He pulled it close to his body, cradling it in his arm like a baby. It shone like a precious and rare jewel. It was beautiful!

Stepping of the last step, Roland stared at it. "What is it?" he whispered reverently.

"A feather," Abadon replied.

"I know it's a feather, I mean, where did it come from?" Roland asked, so spellbound he didn't even roll his eyes at Abadon.

"Phoenix feather it is. Very rare, very powerful."

Roland slowly handed the feather to Abadon, but Abadon shook his head no. Instead, he reached out and opened Roland's coat. Inside, just below Finch's pocket, was another, long enough to fit the full length of the feather. It was as though that pocket had been made with the feather in mind. Come to think of it, Roland didn't remember a pocket like that being there before.

Roland carefully put the feather in, guiding it all the way down until it reached the bottom, completely hidden from view.

Releasing a huge breath, Roland once again clamped his hand over the deep gash in his arm in an attempt to stop the bleeding.

Sir Balkan tore off part of his own sleeve and tied a tourniquet around his upper arm. Nodding his thanks, Roland turned to go. He wanted to get out of this place. Like not now, but right now!

Roland hobbled to the narrow tunnel, passing through it to return to the foul, stinky room. Gagging upon entering, Roland breathed through his mouth in an attempt to filter some of the smell.

Sir Balkan put his armor back on while Abadon approached Pentally and Kentor. Both still stood in the exact same spot as though they had been glued to it. Abadon put his hand on the young centaur's shoulder and spoke quietly.

"How are we going to get out of here," Roland asked Sir Balkan, his voice full of concern. He sure hoped they hadn't come this far only to be trapped in this room, unable to ever escape.

Pulling his sword out, Sir Balkan walked to the doors. Standing in front of them, he was silent for a moment. Then he raised his sword over his head, positioned himself sideways, took three steps back and swung.

Steel on steel screeched out and Roland saw sparks fly. Oh man, that was sweet! The knight had just sliced through the hinges of the doors.

Standing quiet for a moment, Roland held his breath, releasing it slowly when no guards rushed in. Sir Balkan, replacing his sword dug his fingers into the crack between the door and the wall and heaved. It slowly opened, bit by bit as the hinges clanged uselessly against the wood. Again and again Sir Balkan pulled until the space was wide enough for them to fit through.

Stepping out into the darkness of the hallway to make sure the coast was clear, Sir Balkan returned, stood to the side and motioned the dragon to go through first.

Abadon had to restrain Pentally, who did not want to let go of his dead father's hand, but there wasn't room for him to go through at the same time as the dragon. Pentally stood back, shifting impatiently from hoof to hoof until Kentor was on the other side. As soon as he was able, he quickly followed to resume his station beside his father, reaching, finding, and once more, clasping the lifeless hand.

Abadon indicated that Roland should go next. Roland didn't need to be told twice to get out of that room of stink, rot and death.

Abadon then helped Sir Balkan pull the door back into place.

Roland almost growled with impatience, "Come on, let's go you guys!" he said, unable to stand it anymore.

Sir Balkan turned to him and said, "Listen kid, hold your shorts on. If we leave this door wide open, what's going to happen next huh? I'll tell you what, the sand waifs will know right away we escaped, and then they will realize we stole their precious artifact. If the door is closed, do you think they open it to play fetch with their pet?" At Roland's head shake, he continued. "Exactly. Since they gave it a dragon, two centaurs and three people, I reckon they won't feed it again for a month. So unless you want the sand waifs chasing after us sooner than that, we can just leave this door wide open to announce our departure!"

"Oh," said Roland, feeling foolish. "Sorry." He mumbled.

"Yes, well, uh, time to go," Sir Balkan said uncomfortably. He hadn't meant to be so hard on the kid, but he wanted to get out of that stinking hole just as bad as everyone else did, so his patience was a little on the short side.

Finch continued to hover above the group and his light remained strong and true. They had no problem staying together, seeing where they were going or traversing the tunnels below the sand, eventually finding the exit and escaping.

26

Never Forget

The rag tag group never stopped. Sir Balkan led them out of the sand tunnels to the desert surface, and they walked the rest of the night. Finch's fiery ribbons were as bright as a street light.

When the yellow sun eventually peaked over the horizon, Finch fluttered in front of Roland. Seeing exhaustion written all over his face, Roland opened his jacket for Finch. The little fire sprite was so drained, he practically fell inside. Roland decided the little guy deserved a reward and made a mental note to try to find Finch something special to eat if he could. It had obviously taken a lot out of him to keep his light going for as long as he did.

They walked in the sunlight, not stopping until early afternoon when they finally crossed out of the desert, and continued on until they reached a wide, swift flowing river. They all collapsed heavily on the ground in complete and utter exhaustion. Roland was so glad to get out of that desert. He spent the whole time, every single footstep, worried the sand waifs would suddenly spring up and they would be caught again.

After a brief rest, Prince Pentally loving removed his father's crown and beaded necklace. The ground was soft and they all knelt together to dig. No one spoke. King Tartae of the Clan Overon was then buried there beside the river. They left a small marker so that sometime in the near future, Pentally could return and take his father home where he belonged, where his people could honor him and bury him in the way of the centaurs.

Roland didn't feel pain in his arm or leg anymore. Grief overrode all of that, and when they finished pushing the dirt over the royal centaur, they left the king's son to say goodbye in private.

Roland took off his jacket and walked straight into the river, not stopping until he was waist deep. He dunked his head under the water over and over again, trying desperately to wash away the horrors he had seen. The fresh, cold, clean water was not enough though. It would never be enough. Even though his body felt refreshed, his heart and soul felt dusty, weary, old and very sad. He didn't get out until his hands and feet were wrinkled and white.

Abadon tended to Roland's wounds, retrieving his magical liquid with a wave of his hand. The wounds quickly healed. Roland winced at the pain of the muscle and flesh resealing itself. Nothing remained but barely noticeable scars.

"Why didn't you use that stuff to save King Tartae?" asked Roland wearily.

"Good for minor injuries. If full power I had, with this," he said giving the bottle a slight shake, "save him I could. Not enough power in realm is there now. Calling forth Balkan sword used all. If could have saved, would have!"

Lowering his head, Roland realized it was an unfair question. If any of them could have done something to save King Tartae, they would have.

"What do we do now Abadon?" Roland asked. "We have no food, no supplies, no weapons, nothing."

Before Abadon could answer, Sir Balkan approached. Standing over Roland, he stared at the young boy. Roland shifted uncomfortably. Jeez man, what's his problem? Was he still mad at Roland about the door thing?

"Why did your blood free the artifact from the black magic?" he asked suddenly.

Roland was surprised at the question and looked at Abadon. Abadon gave a slight nod.

"Well, because the scroll said only the blood of innocent magic shall pass. I have dragon spirit in me and dragons have their own magic. But since I don't know how to use it, nor have used it, I figured it must still be innocent magic, I guess, in a way," he fumbled, hoping that he was making sense.

Frowning the knight wanted to know how it was possible for Roland to have the spirit of a dragon in him, so Roland told him what had been revealed to him in the mirror.

Astonished, Sir Balkan turned to Abadon. "This is unheard of! This gives me hope Abadon. Kid, you are just full of surprises! You get a handle on that dragon magic you are walking around with, and we just might manage to save this realm."

"Yeah, but easier said than done." Roland replied wearily.

"From what I have seen of you kid, if anyone can pull this off, it will be you." Giving Roland an awkward punch on the shoulder, he turned and walked off.

"Was it okay I told Sir Balkan about the dragon spirit inside me Abadon?"

Abadon looked down at Roland.

"Okay it is. Trust him you can. Why not worried about scrolls Roland, but worry about food?"

Roland plopped backward on the grass to stare up at the sky and closed his eyes. Why? Because he was carrying a secret, a secret about the scrolls, that's why he wasn't concerned about them being destroyed.

Eltanin had sworn him to secrecy about the scrolls. Roland trusted Abadon and wanted very badly to share the secret, but he stiffened his resolve. A promise was a promise, and he had promised Eltanin he wouldn't tell anyone. Unless he had no choice, he was going to keep that secret.

Sitting up, Roland only shrugged his shoulders in response.

"Maybe because I'm starving?" Roland said.

Narrowing his eyes, Abadon said, "Keep your secrets for now if you must. Destroy the scrolls I did not?" Abadon asked, referring to the ones in the jail.

"Well, yes, you did. You destroyed those ones."

"But not real ones they were." Abadon quickly surmised. "Safe the real ones are?"

Roland gave one short curt nod. Yes he had them, and yes they were safe. He just couldn't say where.

"Rest now, read second scroll later," Abadon said before walking away.

Roland lay back down on the soft grass. Pentally was beside his father's grave with his back to Roland. Turning his head sideways, Roland watched the rhythmical steady rise and fall of the centaur's body. He was glad Pentally was sleeping. He figured it probably wasn't a restful sleep but it was sleep nonetheless.

Roland's heart ached for Pentally's loss. He knew what the young centaur was feeling. He had recently gone through the exact same pain and shock when he saw his father and mother turned to stone before his very eyes. He had thought they were dead. He knew if they failed to defeat Rahm, they would be dead, in fact, they would all be dead.

Pentally would never have the hope Roland carried in his heart however. For Pentally, it was over. His father was gone forever.

The last thing he did before closing his eyes was to look over at the newest member of their team. The young dragon, who had begged to come along with them, had not only stolen the Timekeeper but thrown the realm into chaos. And yet, Roland thought to himself, that young dragon had just saved their lives. Something to think about.

Roland closed his eyes and immediately fell asleep.

Eltanin surveyed the scene on the wall. His heart ached for the loss of his old friend, the centaur king. Roland had shown great courage and resourcefulness, and Eltanin's hope bloomed like a flower in spring. Maybe, just maybe, they could defeat the darkness that was at hand.

Realizing the companions would be resting for a while, he decided to take this time to tend to some duties. He needed to ensure the rest of the realm remained unaware of what was at stake.

Before opening the door to his secret chamber, he hesitated. He felt as though someone was watching him. But that was impossible! Glancing around, he just missed seeing two large eyes as they faded from the stone wall across the room.

27

The Black Dragon

Rahm paced in the darkness of the old mountain castle. The Kingdom of Rallag was overcast and filled with an eerie fog. He was angry, and a deep, dark hatred rolled inside him like hundreds of thousands of ants crawling under his skin. A red haze filled his vision.

A disembodied voice floated out of the darkness, echoing and bouncing around the cave walls, "Rahm, they have stolen one of the artifacts and escaped!"

"They will not get far?" he growled.

"They haven't yet read the second scroll. I was almost caught spying on Eltanin. I will continue to watch from his castle but I must be careful. I will let you know when I have more information."

"We must stop them!"

"We will my dark friend, we will. I must go now," the voice said, fading away into the darkness.

The dragon continued pacing. The rage in his heart only continued to grow with each passing moment. Throwing his head back, he roared in frustration. The mountain vibrated and the gargoyle army at the base of the mountain castle, raised their heads.

A quiet stillness filled their camp and they looked to their leader. Grunting, he waved them back to their duties while a restless, anxious pall fell over them all.

An angry dragon was a dangerous dragon.

The voice, hearing his name being called, quickly closed up the small wooden magic sound box he was using to communicate with the dragon. Rising up off the floor, he carried the box over to a small table. Setting it down, he turned his attention to a tapestry on the wall. It was sixteen inches by twenty four inches, depicting the suns alignment and the release of the realm's magic.

Gazing longingly at all that magic, he was snapped out of his daydreams when he heard his name again. He removed the tapestry and carefully laid it on the floor. Retrieving the box, he held it under one arm while he pressed the centre stone. It slid out of the wall like a drawer. He placed the sound box inside, pushed the stone back into the wall and replaced the tapestry

His name reverberated from somewhere in the castle, louder and more demanding, and he hurried from the room. His master was calling, but it wasn't his true master. His true master was dead, killed by the white dragon Chelios, many, many years ago. He would avenge that death. Almost skipping in glee, he couldn't wait until he was the master, and everyone would come running when he called!

Acknowledgements

First, I need to acknowledge a wonderful lady who helped me find a passion for reading when I was very young. Thank you Rita!

To Dalton, for taking the time out of your incredibly busy schedule to read the first draft and give such amazing feedback.

To Sandra, for reading this book almost as many times as I did!

Thank you to my husband Dean for never wavering in his belief this book would be written and published.

Thanks to my kids for just being so amazing and fantastic. I am so proud, and I hope you follow your dreams and find your rainbows.

To my Mom - there are so many things I could list and thank you for but that would be a book unto itself, so in that case, I shall simply say thank you for everything!

Coming Soon ..

Roland's adventures continue in

Suns of Magic

The Dragon Tear

Book II